The Accident of Robert Luman

As a child Robert Luman had been the pride of his parents: good, well mannered, with glowing school reports that gave nothing but praise – *'Robert has worked hard . . . Robert's written work is much improved . . . Well done, Robert'*.

The accident changed all that. Robert's life was irrevocably turned upside down. While his father died, Robert was trapped in a world where fact and fantasy mingled together, but never quite harmonised: cocooned by his mother, Phyllis, partially but never totally understanding everyday life.

Within this half-world, Robert wanted to be famous, recognisable, like Superman and when he saw that girl who had disappeared, Leni Mitchell, on TV and her picture in the paper, he sensed his opportunity. Robert had seen Leni before, the day she went missing. He'd seen her skiving off school, running away. But what else had Robert seen? What had he done? People began to wonder. Where *was* Leni Mitchell?

The Accident of Robert Luman is a tense psychological puzzle, a disturbing and compelling study of the parameters of the human brain. It is a worthy successor to David Fletcher's previous novels, which have included *Rainbows End in Tears* and, most recently, *On Suspicion*, and which are renowned for their attention to detail and perception of character.

THE ACCIDENT OF
ROBERT LUMAN

David Fletcher

MACMILLAN
LONDON

First published in Great Britain 1988 by
MACMILLAN LONDON LIMITED
4 Little Essex Street London WC2R 3LF
and Basingstoke

Associated companies in Auckland, Delhi, Dublin,
Gaborone, Hamburg, Harare, Hong Kong, Johannesburg,
Kuala Lumpur, Lagos, Manzini, Melbourne, Mexico City,
Nairobi, New York, Singapore and Tokyo

British Library Cataloguing in Publication Data
Fletcher, David, 1940–
The accident of Robert Luman.
Rn: Dulan Whilberton Barber   I. Title
823′.914 [F]   PR6056.L43

ISBN 0–333–45781–1

Typeset by Columns of Reading

Printed and bound in the U.K. by
Anchor Brendon Ltd., Essex

For
Colleen and Charles Stuart-Jervis
with love and gratitude

PROLOGUE

Not even the desecration of the garden with its torn-up rose-bushes and resultant drops of blood, like crushed flower petals on the concrete path, could prepare Jolley for what lay inside. The sight of that wiped the smile from his face, a happening that was to be talked about for a long time afterwards. Jolley was famous for his smile if, as he liked to joke, for nothing else. Some maintained it was not a smile at all but an accident of flesh caused by the natural shape of his face and the extra weight he carried. Others claimed that it was a false smile, a studied expression that never lit or softened his eyes. True or false, it was his habitual look, his trademark, and that hazy, mid-week summer morning first Arthur Smith, the village constable, and then David Hughes, Jolley's sergeant, saw his eyes cloud and harden, his jowls droop. Smith actually witnessed the transformation, for he was waiting anxiously inside the bungalow, but Hughes saw the finished mask when Jolley did a sort of double-take, or perhaps he simply averted his eyes for a moment from what he had glimpsed. The look on his face, the absolute absence of his smile was enough to stop Hughes, who had been following him hurriedly, in his tracks.

'Sir?'

Jolley recovered quickly, waved a pudgy hand, the thick wrist of which was incongruously braceleted with a copper band at his wife's insistence, to ward off rheumatism. The gesture, which silenced Hughes and made him peer around the bulk of his superior officer in an attempt to see for himself what had quenched the Jolley smile, also beckoned him to follow silently, with a touch of stealth. His body filling the doorway, Jolley asked the ashen-faced Smith: 'You've touched nothing?'

'No, sir.'

'Close the door, Dave,' he said without looking at Hughes.

1

'And stay by it. Nobody comes in.' This to Smith, who nodded.

The door snicked shut. Jolley's shoulders rolled and heaved beneath the jacket of his summer linen suit, a movement that, in a less fleshy man, would have been instantly recognisable as bracing himself.

'Where is she?' he asked Smith, his voice small and uncertain, betraying that he did not want her to be there at all, or did not wish to see her if she was.

'Well . . . ' Jolley's eyebrows rose instantly. He did not like equivocation, dithering. A simple question deserved a simple answer. 'Sort of . . . everywhere,' Smith said, embarrassed. Jolley frowned, not just with his brows but with all the folds and creases of his face. He looked fearsome. He hesitated a moment, uncomfortably aware that his size made the little hallway cramped, deprived the other men of space, prevented Hughes from taking in the enormity of the situation, Smith from assuming his appointed post. He felt them both impatient, shuffling, but he had to take it in himself first, prepare himself.

The hallway had contained, he remembered clearly, a small crescent-shaped table of frosted glass and ornamental metalwork on which a telephone had stood. Above it a mirror. The hall was too tiny to contain much else, except perhaps a row of wooden pegs on which to hang coats. He looked to his left and saw these. Somehow they had escaped the carnage. The table and the mirror were shards of glass on the floor. The bits of coloured plastic and little black chips that looked like micro-circuits were the remnants of the telephone, he supposed. Where the mirror had hung, an innocent man might have mistaken the blood for a wild streak of red paint. Exhaling audibly, crunching glass underfoot Jolley turned right into the living room.

'What the hell do you mean?' Hughes demanded in a stage whisper of Smith.

'It's true, honest,' Smith said, his voice cracking dangerously.

'Quiet, you two,' Jolley said from the shattered room. 'Show a bit of respect.'

It had had, Hughes saw, a glass door. The splintered frame,

hanging askew, jammed against the carpet, now containing only jagged fragments of glass, held in place by putty that had proved stronger than the blows. Moving forward he could not make sense of the room as Jolley could, who remembered it as cosy and welcoming. Furniture, ornaments, even the shattered television, were piled like the crude beginnings of some terrible bonfire. The pinkish-beige tiles of the fireplace were split and cracked. Some had fallen away revealing brick and plaster and there, set deliberately and neatly on the hearth, was the head of a woman.

'Jesus Christ,' Hughes said, understanding now, with a churning feeling in his stomach, what Smith had meant by his imprecise answer.

'Amen to that,' Jolley said.

She looked younger than she really was, more as she must have been as a girl, Jolley thought. Her hair was still coiled in rollers, though discoloured.

Jolley's arm bumped against Hughes as, with a sudden lunge of energy, he crossed the room to a wooden door which bore the scars of two axe blows. Behind it was a narrow, dark corridor. To the right water spilled from the broken toilet bowl, visible through the open bathroom door. The kitchen, into which Jolley forced his way next, once so pristine and neat, resembled an abattoir. Its main piece of furniture, a plain deal table, solid and four-square, covered in a length of American cloth, bore the woman's armless torso. The sight summoned to Jolley's mind a photograph he had seen in a magazine. A piece of art they'd called it, on display in some German gallery, the manufactured body of some mutilated victim, made out of hessian, plaster and paint. It had had a grisly reality just as this obscenity, he conceded, had some intentional touch of art about it.

Hughes stood back to let him pass, glanced in and coughed to hide the involuntary gasp of shock that rose to his lips. Her bedroom next, the smaller of the two remaining rooms and where, Jolley thought, his mind beginning to work along routine lines again, the carnage might have started. Everything

3

here was smashed, even to the light-fitting which dangled low from the cracked ceiling and the padded bedhead, which spewed forth fluffy stuffing from the rents. And there was a great deal of blood, first blood possibly. A bloodied pink bedroom slipper lay incongruously amid the chaos. Not quite everything was broken, he corrected himself, scouring the room again. A framed photograph had escaped. It leaned against the skirting board in the far corner of the room, a typical family group, stiffly posed but freely smiling, the child sheltered between the two adults, the seated woman and the standing man. The photograph, he knew, had not escaped, had been set there deliberately, out of harm's way, before the killing and the destruction began. Family photos, Jolley thought, are a common kind of totem. This one, simply by its being saved intact took on the force of something primitive, even sacred. What he did not know was whether she, in the final split second before her attacker struck, had placed it there or if the attacker, with reverence and ritual, had removed it out of some terrible pang of humanity almost too dreadful to contemplate, before the axe was raised and brought savagely down.

The photograph brought to mind, in complementary photographic sharpness, the image of his own wife stoutly declaring, in answer to some Christmas parlour game, that if the house were indeed to catch fire and she could save only one object, it would be her photograph albums. That way, she would have a record of her life intact. For a long time after that morning, Jolley was to be haunted by a recurring dream: his wife, wrapped in her cornflower-blue robe, distraught and dishevelled, leaving a burning building, this photograph held out in front of her like an offering. The photograph moved him that much, more even than the wreckage of the last room.

At first glance, it alone seemed less violently changed than the others for it had been crammed, untidy, things all higgledy-piggledy at his only other sight of it. Then, too, the single bed had been unmade, clothing strewn about. But the hacked and broken amplifier had stood upright and too large for the room. The expensive dusty guitar had hung on the wall, not lain like the aftermath of a Who concert. The tennis racket, the golf clubs, the record player and piles of records all lay twisted, smashed and scarred. Even the books and magazines, reminders of some passing enthusiasm that had petered out for lack of concentration, were torn and scrunched up in some terrible act of misplaced self-destruction.

'No blood,' Hughes said, his breath hissing.

There was something else wrong, Jolley thought. The absence of blood was understandable. But something was missing. He could not place it, simply felt it. He shook it off, knowing that this was not the time to worry at details. Probably whatever it was would turn up, buried beneath the piles of broken objects, when the specialists sifted through them. What mattered was, was this room first or last? Had he begun here, rage turned inward which later spilled over, uncontrollable, to the rest of the house, her? Or had this been the final act, an attempt to destroy, symbolically, the destroyer, or to identify with the woman?

'No arms,' Hughes said suddenly. 'We've seen everything else. Where the hell are her arms?' He spoke too loudly, near hysteria, making the location of the arms seem of paramount importance.

'Steady,' Jolley said, but Hughes was already off, retracing their steps, his feet squelching on the carpet as more water seeped from the bathroom. But they were not in the bathroom. Only the cracked walls and shattered bowl, the smashed scales, the splintered cupboard and gooey mess of broken medicine bottles, pills, the reek of cheap cosmetics.

A strangulated cry from the kitchen told Jolley that Hughes had found the arms. Where else should they be but where, probably, they had spent a disproportionate part of their life? The ghost of his smile returned then, unseen, as he recognised in the location of the arms, a certain, tender wit, a scrap of intelligence.

ONE

It was one of those days when Robert had great difficulty making up his mind. When Mam woke him at seven with a cup of tea and his biscuit, he almost decided not to go. He had heard Paula Brownlow moaning on about him having a day out last night: 'It's you that should be having a day out, Phyll, not him. It's you that needs a change.' But he would not change his plans on Paula's account. He got up and he got ready but somewhere inside him he was still undecided. Perhaps if he stayed at home something would happen today.

'Hurry up, son, or you'll miss that bus.'

Mam, he thought, would be upset if he changed his mind, would begin to worry that there was something wrong with him.

It was a quarter of a mile from the bungalow to the main road where the bus stop was and Robert dawdled, not noticing the passage of time or his whereabouts. He progressed by fits and starts, sometimes quickly, sometimes slowly, as did his thoughts. He thought that it was a nice morning, that he had forgotten his money, then felt it bulging out of his inside pocket. He thought that he would miss Wimbledon on the telly and then remembered that he did not like Wimbledon any more. Like so many other things it had become boring. He imagined instead a film he might see when he got to Anderton. He imagined it so clearly, images overlapping, dazzling, the soundtrack throbbing in his ears, his face alternately wreathed in smiles or apprehensive with tension, that when it ended he felt that he had actually seen it. Disappointment clouded him as he realised there would be no point now, none at all, in his paying two quid odd to see it. The day stretched purposeless and he thought he might as well turn back, go home.

Cars whizzed by and lorries. With a slow start, Robert realised that he had reached the main road, was standing on the very kerb while the traffic zoomed past, creating a wind that snapped and tugged at his clothing. The bus shelter was on the other side, a solitary brick and tile building that almost no one ever used now that the bus service had been so drastically reduced and everyone had cars. On this side of the road, where Robert still stood, surprised and uncertain, there was a bus stop but no shelter. The buses on this side of the road were even more infrequent and so a shelter was not deemed necessary. Nor was there a post or sign of any kind. About twenty-five yards to Robert's left was a lay-by, a pale concrete inset which temporarily widened the road and narrowed the footpath and even as he stared at it, blankly, a bus was pulling in, pale blue and yellow. It looked pretty. Robert began to run towards it and arrived panting, heaving himself up the three steep steps to find himself facing a young man he had never seen before.

The bus to Anderton, which he had intended to catch, was invariably driven by an old man with thinning hair and metal-rimmed spectacles. His name was Harold and everyone knew him and greeted him by name. This man was young, with reddish curly hair and a narrow moustache that drooped down the sides of his mouth. Unlike Harold, who always wore a crisp blue shirt and dark blue tie with the name of the bus company woven into it, this man was wearing a purple vest and pop music played softly. The young man looked at Robert with pale grey eyes that had flecks of other colour in them. Robert thought he saw his lips twitch as he surveyed him and spoke quickly, too loudly.

'Return. Please.'

'One pound eighty to you.'

'One forty.'

'That's to Anderton. Other side of the road, mate. Be along in five minutes.'

'I know.' Robert fumbled his purse from his inside pocket, jerking at zips. He counted out the coins slowly into the little black dimpled dish that topped the half-door that shut the driver in. The young man watched him but made no move. 'There,' Robert said proudly. 'One pound, eighty pence.' He was good at sums.

'You sure you don't want to go to Anderton?'

'This bus,' Robert said crossly. 'One pound eighty.' He tapped the black dish, making the coins rattle.

'OK.' With a shrug of his bare shoulders, the young man clicked dials around, wound a handle and a little pink ticket popped out, was torn off and handed to Robert who smiled at it. 'We come back at four,' the driver said and touched something that made the automatic door behind Robert sigh and close.

It was only then, as he started down the gangway, that Robert realised he was the only passenger and that the bus was not a bus at all. It had orange-coloured boxes let into the roof, carpet on the floor and big windows coloured greyish-bluish-black. It was a coach, luxury coach. Robert had been on coaches before, on day trips with Mam and Auntie Meg. Once, long ago, on a very long journey to stay by the sea.

'Great. Dead great,' Robert said, sinking into soft upholstery towards the back of the bus. The ashtrays had lids and Robert rattled one up and rattled it down again, grinning. The pop music played louder now as the bus moved and Robert hummed tunelessly as he fiddled with the ventilators set in a panel above his head. It was a real coach, going somewhere and wouldn't Mam be surprised when he told her?

A cool jet of air playing on his face, Robert settled back, stretching his legs under the seat in front and lit a ciggie from a battered packet zipped into his left-hand pocket. Then he checked his purse, heavy against his heart and stared through the window at the world going by. He dimly remembered Mam and Auntie Meg talking about some new bus service, run by a private company. He remembered a pink leaflet, the same pink as his ticket and wondered where his ticket was and searched furiously for it, finding it at last in his trouser pocket. Then he had to hold the ticket safely and manage his ciggie and get his inside pocket open and the purse out, put the ticket into the empty compartment of his purse, snap it shut, put it back, zip his pocket and his jacket and all the time smoke kept stinging his eyes. But he managed it all and at last settled back with his forearm pressing the bulge of his purse against his chest for extra safe keeping. Effort and anxiety made him sweat. His heart was racing nervously, pumping against the purse. Robert closed his eyes and saw swimming colours, concentric blue circles on a pink ground, growing smaller and overlapping. He opened his eyes as the coach swung off the main road and travelled narrower ones, with hedges on either side, twisting and turning through fields. Robert had no idea where he was or where he was going.

The bus slowed and stopped at an anonymous crossroads and Robert, craning over the high back of the seat in front, watched an old man climb aboard, clutching a plastic bag. When the coach started again he read some of the names on the white signpost and recognised them. They were places his mother, Auntie Meg and Paula Brownlow often spoke about. The three women talked together about people, people who lived in these places as well as their own village. Sometimes it seemed to Robert, listening, that they must, between them, know someone everywhere. The bus lumbered through a village, stopped again and Robert memorised its name. His mam knew someone here and so, he supposed, in a way, did he. If anyone were to ask him he could say he knew someone who lived there and that would be all right. It was the same at the next two villages and with the names that recurred on the signposts. All were places the women mentioned and which had lodged in his mind through repetition. He realised then that there was no need to memorise the names. He already knew them and could trot out any combination of them and Mam would immediately know where he'd been.

Without this distraction, he was bored. The coach meandered on, looping back and forth. Robert recognised places they had already been to and felt slightly cheated when, crossing the main road again, they began visiting villages he knew by more than name, because they were so close to his own. He tried to look at the other people on the bus – there were quite a lot by now – but the high, comfortable seats made this difficult. He had to be content with scrutinising newcomers as they got on, but the stops became fewer and farther between. The countryside was familiar and all the same, without interest. Now he could not hear the pop music properly because of the chatter of women. Most of the passengers were women. Robert closed his eyes and listened to the meaningless jumble of sound, not even trying to pick fragments of conversation or phrases of familiar music from the muddle. Quite quickly, he fell asleep.

When Robert woke with a little snuffling snore, his chin wet with dribble, they were passing a row of uniform, semi-detached houses on one side and the flat, chimney-dominated stretches of a brickfield on the other. He took out his handkerchief and wiped his chin, blew his nose for good measure and lit another ciggie, thinking that he must buy some more as soon as he got to wherever he was going. There were more people on the bus now and he twisted round to look at a row of loud lads on the backseat, talking and laughing and pushing each other. He grinned. Two of them stared back, eyes narrowed and flicking. Robert turned away quickly and shrank down in his seat, his knees pressed hard against the back of the seat in front. He heard the word 'wally' and pretended he hadn't, puffing greedily on his cigarette.

There were shops now, dusty suburb shops with a run-down air. Newsagents and betting shops, a launderette with two swollen women in summer maternity dresses talking outside. The coach was held up by road works, a single set of temporary traffic lights which took forever to change. Then they whizzed by a deep trench in the road, shirtless men in orange trousers and the rat-a-tat-tat of a pneumatic drill. Robert sensed a restlessness among the passengers, a gathering together of bags and clothing shed against the warmth, the preparations for arrival. He set about making himself ready, checking his cigarettes and his lighter, that his pink return ticket was safe in his purse, the purse itself and zipped up all his pockets safely. He was impatient now, wanted to be off. The coach rode new roads and swung around roundabouts. He saw tall buildings and a confusion of signs. One said 'Bus Station Only' and Robert was up and in the gangway, nearly losing his footing as the bus lurched around a corner. People looked at him. He heard loud laughter behind. Ahead of him others began to rise and squeeze into the gangway, and Robert hurried towards them, pushing. Somebody told him to wait, sharply, but he took no notice and when the doors sighed open, Robert, with a feeling of achievement, was the first off the bus and began limping away quickly.

The limp was so much better now that he forgot about it for days, even weeks at a time. It was only when he had been sitting for very long periods, as now, that his left leg seemed floppy below the knee and he had to remember to think to lift it up and make it go straight. Consequently, he seemed to hop and lurch his way out of the bus station, moving too quickly for his body's comfort. The boys, who had crowded off the bus after him, stood and watched, laughing. Robert knew they were there and hurried from them, willing his leg to obey him, get better again. In this preoccupation, he failed to notice the sign saying 'Town Centre' with an arrow to point the way. It was very hot and he was sweating when he came to a stop at a pedestrian crossing and realised that he did not know where he was. A car stopped and he had to go across, limping. On the other side there were two roads he could take. One offered nothing more than dull, terraced houses, neat gardens. The other was long and straight with tall trees growing on either side, offering shade. Robert hurried towards it and stopped beneath the first tree. Looking back he could see no sign of the boys or, indeed, of anyone he recognised from the coach. He felt better then and walked more slowly, his leg growing stronger all the time.

The avenue of trees on his right stopped suddenly, like a curtain pulled aside to show the dazzling new building set on a little hillock of grass which sloped down to the road where a metal barrier stood to prevent children running into the traffic. Sunlight dazzled from the many black windows and the yellow brickwork. The pointed low roofs looked as fresh and new as they had many years ago when Robert had been a pupil there. The buildings slowly, slowly became familiar and, miraculously, did not even look smaller. They still daunted and excited Robert as they had that softer sunlit morning when, clutching his father's hand, stiff in his thick new blazer, he had climbed the shallow concrete steps towards those yawning doors. He could still smell the woman's perfume and see the blankness of her glasses turned into the sun as she said, 'Don't worry, Mr Luman. We'll take good care of Robert, won't we, Robert?'

Passing cars, shining in the sunlight, shattered his memory. He saw children now streaming between the spaced buildings and could remember precisely the shrill of the bell that put an end to a lesson, signalled playtime, the start of another lesson. Because of the weather, the blue blazers were not worn. Boys in shirt sleeves swung bags. Tidy little girls in blue skirts and patterned blue blouses, the chime of their voices sounding across the road and the traffic to where Robert stood, transfixed, knowing, with a certainty rare for him, exactly where he was. The children split into groups, their paths crossing and fading, and then vanished into buildings like counters on a green board, suddenly swept clean. He took an urgent step forward, teetered on the brink and withdrew, frightened by the rush of cars, by the knowledge that he could not join those children, become a part of that mass again as he had once been.

He walked very slowly now, dragging his feet in the pavement dust, feeling the heat on his back and shoulders. Later, of course, he had gone to the Big School and with pleasure he remembered where that was situated. It was not on the main road but in a quieter, narrower one that wound downhill towards a distant river. Robert almost passed the top of that road, not recognising a new building where he remembered a field. The road was pinkish, newly surfaced, and the banks that rose on either side, making it a sort of sunken secret tunnel, were topped with houses, bright in their newness, beautiful with flowers. Their modernity and richness impressed Robert and he forgot his purpose, twisting round, straining to see their painted wood and stucco wonders. It was voices that pulled him back, reminded him. A group of boys, one pushing a drop-handled racer, advanced up the hill, approached him. Their shirts so white, the bright blue blazers carried by loops over their shoulders. And trailing behind them, girls in fashionable blue skirts and crisp white blouses. Robert smiled with recognition and pleasure but no one smiled back.

He went on, his feet braced against the steep slope of the road. Where it turned a low stone wall began and ran, he knew, straight along where the road levelled and became flat and straight. Beside the stone wall, craggy and old, was a narrow footpath and there, on the other side of the road, looming over everything, was the Big School. A much older building with turrets and gables and bright white bars at the upper windows. A thick green hedge, taller than a man, masked the lower floors. From the driveway, which was marked in shiny studded letters against reflecting blue, 'Caution Children Crossing', more young people came in groups, crossed the road and ambled towards him. A boy walked with his arm around a girl's shoulder. As they squeezed past a stationary, gazing Robert, he saw streaks of colour in the boy's hair, make-up on the girl's face. He smiled at them and said, 'Hello,' to another group. A girl with frizzy hair smiled back, then burst into giggles, trotted, squealing, to catch up with her friends who turned and looked and giggled louder. Robert did not mind. He felt their giggles were welcoming.

He leaned against the warm stone of the wall and admired the building. Faintly, a piano sounded on the heavy air, and treble voices rose in do-re-mi-fa-so steps. He remembered music with Mr Bannister and French with Miss Smith. He remembered that he had done well at the Big School. *Robert is a bright boy and works hard. Robert has made good progress this term. Robert is finding it easier to socialise now that he has settled in.* Best of all, *Well done, Robert!*

He turned his back on the Big School, settled his folded arms as comfortably as possible on the sharp crags that topped the stone wall. The field of long grass below and in front of him was more silver than green and a faint breeze, unnoticed before, stirred it like a liquid, making it change colour, moment by moment. At the bottom of the field, trees rose, much larger and thicker than he remembered. They hid the river and he minded that, remembering the black snake of it, glinting in the sun so that you had to scrunch your eyes up and see how long you could stare at its flash and dazzle. You had to do it until your eyes misted and watered, as his eyes were watering now, for no reason. He sniffed and wanted to put his head down on his arms and weep but knew that he must not, that such behaviour attracted attention, bad words, anger. The field melted and shimmered and shifted in front of him, was as liquid as the river but softer, soothing. Robert pulled his handkerchief from his trouser pocket and wiped his face, blew his nose and, turning a little to find the opening in his trouser pocket, saw the girl.

She ran lightly across the road, her pretty hair bouncing against her shoulders and back. She stopped on the pavement and looked back, looked up at the Big School anxiously. For a moment she hesitated, hands braced against the top of the wall. Robert stared at her, feeling uncomfortable, afraid, suddenly, that the girl might come up to him, speak to him. He began to search for his ciggies, patting his pockets, fiddling with the zips. The girl lifted herself up by her strong arms and swung one leg onto the top of the wall. Robert, holding his cigarettes and lighter tightly, saw the flash of her pale leg, right up into the shadow of her skirt. Such sights made him nervous. He looked away, unconsciously crushing the cigarette packet. The girl half-sat, half-lay on the wall then suddenly pushed free, dropped from sight. Robert, startled, leaned over the wall, saw her hit the ground, slip and tumble. He saw her skirt thrown up, right up and the pale pink of her knickers tight across her bottom. The sight of it all made him laugh out loud. The girl, scrambling to her feet, tossing back her hair and brushing down her skirt, stared at him for a moment, a proper stare, her eyes piercing him. Then she made what Robert knew to be a very rude gesture and turned away, strode through the long grass, away from him.

She didn't ought to do that. It wasn't nice, wasn't called for. It wasn't his fault she'd fallen and showed her knickers. He felt

14

the cigarette packet in his left hand, felt the shreds of coarse tobacco sticking to his damp fingers, and stared at its ruin, growing more angry. Now he was out of ciggies and it was all her fault. He had a good mind to shout at her, to jump over the wall and catch her up and give her a good telling off. For two pins . . . He was hurrying now, along beside the wall, threw the crushed cigarette packet furiously from him into the field. She had no right. Girls shouldn't behave like that, shouldn't. But no matter how he hurried, the girl drew further away from him, on a right-angled course through the edge of the field, towards the trees. Robert stopped, panting, and watched her with a scowl. She had no right in that field. What was she doing in that field, anyway? She ought to have been in school. Playing hookey. He felt a sort of triumph at discovering the extent of the girl's wickedness. She'd get into trouble. She'd get detention, lines, perhaps even a note home.

' . . . *that you should come and talk to me about Robert's behaviour recently . . .* '

She'd get done by the farmer for trampling his hayfield. Everyone knew you mustn't walk in a hayfield, flatten it.

'Want to come in the long grass, Robert? Come on, Robert. Come and lie down in the long grass. We've got something to show you, haven't we, lads?'

She'd get a smack for that, a caning, a right belting and it would serve her right, giving him two fingers like that, showing her knickers like that. She had no right, oughtn't to be there, was a bad girl.

'Bad boy. Bad boy.'

' . . . *Robert's not a bad boy and this is a very difficult time for him, for all young men, for that is how we must now think of him . . .* '

Boy. He saw the boy, then, clear as daylight, sharp against the trees where he must have been waiting, from the shade of which he was now emerging, signalling to the girl. Robert stopped and Robert smiled. He knew. He understood. He looked around him, up and down the road, thought that he was entirely alone. He pressed himself against the wall and watched, watched the girl break into a sort of run, her legs impeded by the long grass, and saw the boy saunter, bold as brass, towards her. Robert began to giggle then. In the woods. He knew what that meant. He knew what they were up to. Go on, son, give her one. He laughed, spluttering, holding his belly as though it ached. Saw the boy meet the girl and fold his arm around her shoulder. For a moment they both looked back at him and he wanted to put two fingers up but could not because he was laughing so much. Then they turned, heads bent close together, and went towards the woods. Can't wait, he thought. Can't wait to do it to her in there. In the woods.

They were gone, into the woods, only the trail of flattened silver grass to show they had ever existed. Robert's laughter sounded silly to his own ears and he stopped it as suddenly as it had begun. He straightened up, fiddling with the white plastic lighter he still held in his hand. Good riddance to bad rubbish, he thought. Dirty devils. His stomach rattled and grumbled with emptiness. He was hungry, wanted a big plate of chips and sausages, lots of HP sauce and two slices. More than that, he thought, hurrying now along the deserted road, he was dying for a ciggie.

He had three sausages, a greasy egg that looked like a daisy and a mound of crisp, brown chips. He ate hunched over his plate, his elbows sticking out and working furiously as he shovelled the food into his mouth. When he had mopped the last vestiges of sauce and yolk and fat from the plate he sat back and belched quietly. He felt better, contented, ordered a second cup of tea and lit a ciggie. His surroundings were red and dirty white, drab. Over the net curtain which veiled the lower portion of the café window, Robert slowly, uncertainly recognised the railway station. He remembered going from there somewhere. It surprised and pleased him how much he remembered of this town so long forgotten. He could not wait to tell Mam. She was always pleased when he found things in his mind. His smile wavered. He fiddled with the pepper and the salt and the sauce bottle, jumbling them in the centre of the table. He slopped his tea as he lifted his cup, making a puddle on the flowered oilcloth. Obscurely, he knew that Mam would not like these memories. She would not like him coming here at all. Robert immediately became agitated, stood up too quickly, knocking the table and making the pepper and salt and sauce bottles rattle together. He saw a large blonde woman bearing down on him, damp cloth at the ready, and he sidled to the door. A little bell went 'ting' when he opened it and for a moment he was numbed by the noise and heat outside which seemed to pin him to the Station Café doorway.

He was scared, knew that he should never have changed his mind, come here. The important thing was to get away as quickly as possible. He need not tell Mam at all. Dithering, shifting from one foot to the other, Robert's mind refused to yield up two salient pieces of information: the time of his return bus and the location of the bus station. His face contorted with anxiety and distress and knowing how he must look, he covered all but his eyes with both hands and stood there, trembling. Slowly the trembling fit passed and his hands felt damp with dribble, but more importantly he saw the railway station opposite and understood its purpose. When he had mopped his face and wiped his hands, looked both ways for traffic, Robert crossed the road and the cobbled station yard and went into the booking hall. He could not make sense of the timetable. All those tiny figures and symbols and abbreviated names danced and slid together. He very badly wanted to go to the lavatory. Mam said, if you don't think about it, you won't want to go, so he tried not to. He turned his back on the timetable and stared nervously at the special window where tickets could be bought. With a fierce effort of concentration, Robert prepared himself. He took out his purse and held it tight in his hand. He mopped his face and blew his nose and tried to make a pleasant smile. He waited for a woman who trailed a child by the hand to complete her business at the window. He used the time to fix in his mind what he must say and saying it stooped close to the window, bought his ticket. Then, fumbling his change, he had to ask when the train left and from where. The man answered

17

gruffly, with impatience, then looking at Robert closely, said the man at the gate would tell him.

The man at the gate said: 'You've got to wait. You can get a cup of tea on platform five. Yours goes from number three. Have you got that? Number three,' and he rolled the gate back and let Robert onto the grey platform. 'Up there and over the bridge. Number three.' The man pointed him in the right direction and Robert saw the sign that promised rescue: 'Gentlemen'.

Robert, relieving himself, realised he had been very clever. He had a ticket in his pocket to Oversleigh, the town nearest his village. Oversleigh had a tiny station that Robert had often passed but never used. From there he could walk home. There were no buses. He knew that. All that made him feel clever, a sense of achievement at having worked it out and got through the most difficult part all by himself. But there was more. This way – and he chuckled at his own cleverness – he would not have to tell Mam that he had ever been to the town. He could say . . . He could say . . . Robert's eye was caught by a rude, a very rude word someone had scrawled on the wall. It glared at him with an ugly belligerence and Robert saw and remembered himself flung against a similar wall, pinned there by a hand pressing at his throat. He saw faces, mean and threatening, surrounding him.

'You ever let on what happened, you mention us and we'll get you, wanker. D'you understand?'

''Cos you're in dead trouble, aren't you, Luman? But you won't tell on us, will you?'

''Cos if you do we'll cut it off, right, lads?'

'Yeah, we'll cut it off, wanker.'

Spittle on his face and the sudden terrible pain in his groin as a knee jabbed there savagely, killing him.

Robert bent over the trough, clutching himself, his forehead resting against the wall. He felt sick and terribly scared. He just wanted to get away as quickly as possible. He fumbled with his clothes, gulping for breath, the terror still real. He didn't understand. Why had they taken him into the long grass then

18

and smiled at him? Why pick on him? Why, if they were afraid? Why, if they hated him so much? Why did they want to hurt him?

Footsteps approached and because of them Robert saw where he really was. He averted his eyes from the word on the wall and from the man who entered with a purposeful tread. Robert checked his zip, his purse, his ticket and went out. He felt weak and tired, wished he was at home in his own room and could curl up with a pillow over his head, safe. He wanted to sit down. Benches beckoned but he remembered that the man at the gate had said number three. If he sat there, even for a minute or two, just to rest, the man would think him stupid or disobedient and come to move him on to the right place. So Robert made himself climb the stairs to the bridge, holding tightly to the rail and almost pulling himself up. At the top, feeling dizzy, he fixed his eyes on the big black '3' where it hung on a white board and went towards it, limping. It was easier going downstairs. The platform was narrow, two platforms, really, with four on one side and three on the other. Robert sat on the first bench he came to and leaned forward, his head in his hands.

The accident happened after Robert's father had visited the Big School, summoned there by a note home which had, by its very existence, charged the atmosphere with tension and anger. Mam's and Dad's loud, frightened voices had sounded long into the night, after he had gone to bed afraid.

After the interview, during most of which Robert had sat on a hard chair outside the headmaster's study, an object of derision and speculation and giggles from passing pupils, his father had led him to the big blue van in which he delivered fruit and vegetables to outlying villages and small towns, while Mam minded the shop in Bridge Street. He waited, small beside the cab, until Dad opened the door for him and then he climbed slowly in and sat dumbly, staring at the windscreen. Robert remembered the big wipers swishing back and forth, back and forth, and his father leaning forward, craned to see the traffic as

19

the blunt-nosed van – *Luman's Fruit and Veg* – peeped shyly out of the driveway. He remembered the wipers and his father sitting bolt upright then, clutching the wheel tightly with his heavy hands.

'I don't know what to say to you. I didn't know what to say to him. I said, "Our Robert? Are you sure you've got the right lad?" I mean, I couldn't think it could be right, could be you. I still can't, and with all those kids, well, it's a wonder they know half of you. But he swore it was you. "No mistake, Mr Luman. I do assure you." I couldn't believe my ears. I still can't. Haven't you got anything to say for yourself?'

The wipers swishing. It seemed to be dark. Perhaps it was winter or the interview had dragged on until sunset. It seemed a wrong dark, storm dark. The lights making glistening splashes on the road, sometimes seen clearly, sometimes fuzzy and indistinct, depending on the position of the wipers.

'That any son of mine . . . I mean, I've thought about it. I know we haven't said much, your mam and me, but we're not stupid. She thinks it's a father's place and maybe she's right. I mean, if you'd been a girl, well, that's women's business, best left to the mother when the time comes. But boys are different. I mean, there's not the necessity . . . But I'd thought, you know, there'd come a time when, well, you'd show an interest in girls and then I'd, like, give you a few pointers. I mean, it's not as though I hadn't thought. And your mam. But this, this beats me.'

The rain drumming on the roof of the van. The smell of old potatoes, soil and, for some reason, of sharp pineapple. A Christmassy kind of smell. It was warm in the cab which juddered as they waited for a gap in the traffic, to turn.

'I mean, whatever possessed you, Robert? Where did you learn such tricks? Not at home, that I do know.'

A horn blaring, a rush of lights. His father's tight-lipped curse.

'Oh, I don't know. I just don't know. I mean, it can only be wickedness or something wrong with you. Is there something wrong with you?'

'I didn't know it was wrong. I didn't.'

'Didn't know it was wrong? What are you talking about? We've brought you up properly. We never taught you to go dancing about in your birthday suit, showing yourself off to the other lads. I've never heard of such a thing. Never. I can't credit it. And as for grabbing at . . . other boys' private parts, well . . . It sickens me. I can't bear to think about it. And all you can say is, you didn't know it was wrong.'

But it wasn't, hadn't been in the long grass when the five of them had held him down and pulled down his clothes and laughed. It hadn't been wrong when they had made him touch them. 'Go on, Robert. It's all right. Go on, Robert.' It hadn't been wrong. It hadn't.

'Well, you'll soon bloody well know that it is wrong. I'll see to that. And that's a promise. I'll beat it out of you if I have to. Mark my words. Didn't know it was wrong. God Almighty.'

The road, narrow and dark with hedges, the rain beating the wipers so that everything was seen through a sheet of running water and the van bounced on pot-holes and swayed with speed and the man's terrible, bewildered anger.

'What pains me most is what this'll do to your mother. She'll have to be told. She's worried out of her mind as it is. This'll kill her. It'll break her heart for sure. I don't know how I'm ever going to tell her. She thinks the world of you, you know, worships you. This'll kill her and it'll all be your . . . '

The horse box came out of nowhere, large and lurching, its lights pinning Robert to his seat. He remembered everything tilting to the right and the unbearable, unforgettable scream of horses.

When he woke there was a terrible pain in his left leg and it was all stiff with plaster. But that was nothing to the pain in his head. He was sick a lot. And the pain in his head went on, got worse, then very gradually better.

A long time later, when Robert began to understand things again, though in little pieces and differently, he had heard talk of brain damage and laughed. He heard that his father might have stood a chance if the accident had happened on a busier or

21

more populated road. As it was, lying there so long . . . Both the horses had had to be put down.

Robert's head ached with a dull pulse. He looked longingly across at platform five where he could see, through a big window, a woman in a pink overall standing beside a silver tea urn, an array of thick white cups laid out before her. He could go a cup of tea, right enough, but he did not dare to leave platform three. He had forgotten what time his train was due and could not summon the courage to ask again. He stared across the empty lines to platform five, stared at a little boy in shorts, collecting train numbers. The boy stared back and when Robert smiled stuck his tongue out. Robert turned his head away, offended. He managed to light a ciggie even though his hands were trembling. He tried to remember where he had bought the ciggies and could not. Already the day was fading from his mind, leaving a feeling of discomfort and apprehension. The ciggies were Marlboro, the man's cigarette. He put them away safely, took his ticket out of his pocket to examine it. It was green with pale red letters. The man at the gate had put a triangular hole in it, through which Robert tried to squint, to frame and reduce the world to a single triangle. Then he remembered and took out his purse, transferred the pink ticket to his pocket, put the green one safely inside the purse and zipped up his pocket again. He sat there, hands tapping on his knees, blank until an elderly diesel wheezed into the station. 'Got your ticket? Good lad. Come on. This one's yours.' The man at the gate propelled him towards the train, holding his elbow. 'Five stops. Got that? Five stops before yours.' He slammed the door on him. 'Don't forget to get off, now, will you?'

This was such a crazy idea, such a daft and delightfully funny idea, that Robert roared with laughter. Long after the train had hooted its way out of the station, Robert shook with laughter. Don't forget to get off. That was a good one. He must tell Mam. She'd laugh. She liked a good laugh. Then Robert put his feet up on the seat opposite, his hands thrust deep into his trouser

22

pockets, and played with himself happily until it was time to get off.

Just outside Oversleigh there was a narrow bridge, so narrow that the traffic had to be controlled by lights, reduced to a single, alternating flow. Robert was studying the lights, wondering how they were able to change so neatly and regularly when Mr Cartwright drew up beside him and said: 'Hello, Robert. Hop in. We'll soon have you home.'

Robert could not handle the seatbelt so Mr Cartwright did it for him. Robert grinned.

'So where have you been, young man?'

'Out.'

'Nice, was it?'

'Great.'

'Why were you walking home, then? Miss the bus, did you?'

'No buses Wednesday.'

'Nor there isn't. You must have been to Anderton, then.'

'Yes.'

'Shopping, was it?'

'Walking round. Having a good time. Great.'

'That's nice. Must've missed the through bus, though. That gets to the village about half four, doesn't it?'

'Yes.'

'Hope your mum's not too worried, eh?'

'Had chips. Great big – great big pile chips. Three sausages.'

'Did you, now? Well, you'll not be hungry, then. Know how to look after yourself, don't you, Robert?'

'Yeah.'

Phyllis Luman opened the front door of the bungalow as soon as she saw Ken Cartwright's car draw up. She looked, fleetingly, worried, but her smile was warm and ready as she came down the path to the gate.

'Hang on a minute,' Cartwright said, as the silly great lump of a man or boy – you really didn't know what to call him – tried to get out of the car without undoing the seatbelt. 'There, off you go.'

He was all over Phyllis, yelling, 'Mam, Mam! Hello, Mam,' and kissing her noisily. She held him tight, smiling at Ken over his shoulder. Then with a pat she sent him off towards the front door and came closer to the car.

'Thanks, Ken.'

'You all right?'

'Yes. I suppose he must have missed the bus.'

'Well, he doesn't seem to have come to any harm.'

'Oh, no.' She turned, watched her son fondly as, swaying a little, ungainly, he disappeared into the house. 'There's not much wrong with my Robert,' she said. 'Thanks again.'

'That's all right, Phyll. You take care, now.'

'And you.'

She paused for a moment at the gate, the sun touching her thick grey hair with colour, and raised her hand in a grateful salute.

TWO

Superintendent Tait was a very tall man of exceptional neatness. His short white hair always looked, to Detective Inspector Riley, to have been parted with a Stanley knife and a set square. Along the furrow of his parting his scalp showed very pink, as pink as his face, which always had a sort of sheen to it as though he had not simply washed but scrubbed and polished himself, too. The Superintendent was a stickler for paperwork and possibly the only thing he had in common with Riley was that the latter was known to prefer to read than to listen. As a consequence of this preference, the report open before the Superintendent was full and as clear as Riley's editorial skills, the writing talents of his men and the availability of an overworked typist could make it. The Superintendent, reaching the bottom of the first page, the corner of which he held poised for turning between the thumb and index finger of his left hand, looked at Riley, who could scarcely have made a greater contrast. Hair too long, slumped in his chair with tie awry and jacket crumpled, obviously pulled on in haste because he was going to see 'the old man'. Shirt bloused over trousers which, the Superintendent recalled, he had an irritating habit of hitching constantly. Riley returned his gaze and, as though he could read the criticism behind the bland friendly expression, refused to sit up or straighten his tie. The Superintendent looked down at the report again.

'The girl would appear to be called Lenora Mitchell. This "Leni" – is that some kind of diminutive?'

'That's what they call her, sir. For short.'

'I see. Where do they get these names, I wonder?' The question, to which in any case Riley had no answer, was evidently rhetorical, since the Superintendent hurried on in a flat monotone. 'Lenora Mitchell was marked absent at afternoon

25

registration on the twenty-fifth by the form teacher, Mrs Patricia Quentin. No one in the class knows anything about her absence. The teacher then questioned one . . . Tracy Vorlander?' He looked up again, his eyes wide with surprise.

'The Mitchell girl's best friend,' Riley said quickly, fearing that the Superintendent would expand and draw out the theme of names.

'Good Heavens. Do they still have "best friends", girls?' he said dreamily, lingering on the word 'girls' as though it carried a scent that tantalised and drew him back into some private world. 'I don't see that interesting fact noted here. It might be as well . . .'

'Further on, sir. When the girl was interviewed a second time . . .' Riley leaned forward, reached towards the folder, seeing a chance, perhaps, to speed this tedious process up and make the old man get to the bloody point, but the Superintendent would have none of it. He flattened his left hand on the report and looked reprovingly at Riley, this time over the frame of his bifocals.

'All right, Inspector. All in good time.'

Riley slumped back in his seat, hitched his left ankle onto his right knee and contemplated a stain – oil, by the look of it – on his short blue nylon sock.

'But Tracy Vorlander was unable to assist Mrs Quentin and nothing further seems to have taken place. Indeed,' he said, speeding up now, flipping over the page and running his finger down the second, 'it would appear from this that no one actually showed any concern about the girl's absence until three forty-five on the following day. That would be the twenty-sixth.'

'Yes, sir.'

'Extraordinary.' The Superintendent read for a little, lips pursed. 'The girl was again marked absent from school. Miss Vorlander, in her capacity of best friend, was again questioned, whereupon the good Mrs Quentin telephoned the girl's home. Receiving no reply, she contacted the school secretary, one Mrs Fancy – what extraordinary names all these people have, Inspector. I would have thought to be called Mrs Fancy was a liability. Mrs Fancy, however, provided Mrs Quentin with a second telephone number, that of the mother's workplace.' Again he read, turned the page, read on. 'She doesn't appear to have been unduly worried.'

'No, sir. Not according to the teacher's account.'

'That would be the unfortunately named Mrs Fancy?'

'No, sir. Mrs Quentin.'

'Ah, yes, quite so.'

Just testing, Riley thought. He was going to make a meal of it, question every comma, correct any slovenly grammar that had slipped past Riley's own less than eagle-sharp eye. The trouble with the Super was, he fancied himself as a judge. The whole boring, time-wasting process was an act, intended to test and annoy. For two pins . . .

'What's the home background like?' the Superintendent asked suddenly, cutting through Riley's mounting anger with the sort of incisiveness that had earned him his rank and which now, concealed under his meticulous, bumbling-judge pose, he used as a weapon.

'Well, sir . . . ' Riley said, sitting up and pulling his tie a little straighter.

The mother was hard-faced and too blonde. Riley had heard talk about her and was inclined to believe it. The estranged father looked more like a weasel than a stud though he was known to be living with a girl half his age on the Anderton Road.

'So, you've no reason to think she was upset and you've no idea where she is?'

'I told you, I thought she was with Tracy or at Michelle's. But she'll be home. She'll be all right. I know my Leni and I think you're all making a lot of fuss about nothing.'

'But she has been reported missing . . . '

'Oh, that school. Yes, well, I mean, they can't keep 'em in order for five minutes. It's a disgrace. And all they do is blame the parents.'

'These days,' the husband put in, 'you can't be too careful . . . '

'You'd know, would you?' She rounded on him with an almost dignified turn of the head. 'Well, yes, I suppose you would in some ways, but what you know about my Leni . . . ' He opened his mouth to protest or bring her back to the point, perhaps, but nothing came out. 'When did you even see her last? Christmas, was it?' The man, Mitchell, subsided into the corner of the room. Satisfied, she turned back to Riley. 'You'd be better off checking with her friends.'

'We have. Those we know. She didn't spend the night with anyone at the school. No one there has seen her since eleven twenty-five Wednesday morning. You tell me about her friends.'

She looked outraged at this.

'Well, I don't know. I've got a job, three kids and no man to support me. If you think I've got time to keep tabs on Leni's friends, you're living in cloud-cuckoo-land.'

'Boyfriends?' Riley suggested, keeping his eyes on his notebook.

'Well, I don't know . . . '

'Then you bloody well ought,' Mitchell said, roused from his corner.

'Just a minute! Don't you "ought" me . . . '

'All right, all right.' Riley stood up, dwarfing her as she rose, belligerent, from her chair. She glared at him but sat down again. 'If we could just keep calm and concentrate on your daughter.'

'Well, tell him to keep his trap shut, then.'

Riley looked at Mitchell who shrugged, hunched his shoulders and stared out of the window.

'Boyfriends?' Riley repeated.

'There was no one special, if that's what you mean. My Leni's too sensible to go tying herself to one man. But, of course, she was very popular . . . ' At last names began to emerge and Riley dutifully jotted them down. Most of them were boys at the school, some of whom had already been questioned. They would have to double-check on those she named, lean on the others a bit. A chore, he thought, that would probably lead nowhere.

28

'Mr Mitchell, did she ever say anything to you about a boy, a special boy?'

'No. I haven't seen her much lately . . . '

'That's the understatement of the year,' the mother snorted. To Riley she confided, 'They don't communicate. Never have. He's not got time for kids. Not his own, anyway.' Mitchell shrugged again.

'What about her brother and sister? Does she confide in them?' Riley said, knowing he was beginning to sound desperate.

'Search me. I shouldn't think so. Not Wayne, anyway. They don't hit it off. You know how kids are at that age. And my Linda's only a baby . . . '

'Are they here?'

'I should bloody hope not. Wayne's at work, Ellison's Garage, and Linda's at school. And I've got a job to go to, you know. Somebody's got to keep the roof over our heads.'

He wound it up then with the usual reminder to let them know if Leni showed up or they heard anything at all. Mitchell, looking less hunted, preceded him to the front door where, with a jerk of her head and a touch on Riley's arm, the mother detained him. Mitchell walked on out, as though not interested.

'Look, I'm not indifferent. I don't want you to think that. Truth is, I'm worried sick, but I can't be myself in front of him. Don't bring him here again, all right?' Riley nodded. 'The thing is, I trust my Leni. That's how I've brought all my kids up, to be open, responsible, trusting. You know what I mean? She wouldn't do anything daft. And if there was anything wrong, she'd tell me. People often say we're more like sisters.' Here she simpered and fluffed at the waves of her bright blonde hair.

'So where do you think she is, then?' Riley said, watching the flash of annoyance in her eyes as he failed to pick up on the 'sisters' remark.

'I don't know. Cross my heart . . . But she won't have done anything bad or stupid. And if anything's upset her, it's him, him and his teenage fancy piece.'

Mitchell was waiting for him on the pavement.

'All my bloody fault, I suppose?' he said, rolling his eyes towards the house.

'Something like that. You got anything to add?'

'Nothing useful. Christ, you've got to find her. You see it every day in the papers, on the telly, kids half her age . . . I tell you, I'm worried. Sheila's right about one thing, though. She's a good kid, something's happened to her . . . '

'It would help,' Riley said, 'if we had something to go on. If you think of anything or she contacts you . . . '

'Yeah, yeah. Right. But do us a favour, will you? Find her. That's all I ask.'

'So it would seem,' Superintendent Tait said, leaning back in his chair and making a skeletal tent of his fingers, 'that you only have little Miss Vorlander's "funny man" to go on.'

Riley was stung by the subtly stressed 'you', wanted to say, We're all in this, all of us, and while we're on the subject, Tracy Vorlander is a thick fat slob.

'So it would seem, sir,' he said with heavy irony. If the Superintendent noticed this, he chose to ignore it.

'Quite. What I don't understand is why your young informant didn't come straight out with it at her first interview.'

'Oh, you know how kids are, sir. Afraid of ratting on a mate, getting a friend into trouble,' he amended slightly, to avoid another discourse on language.

'My point is, should you not treat Miss Vorlander's second statement with . . . caution? The girl had had time to invent something.'

'Or to remember, sir.'

'The description is somewhat . . . redolent of the yellow press, is it not?' He bent over the relevant sheet, read with an audible distaste, 'Funny, staring eyes.'

'I don't think the girl has any other vocabulary, sir.'

Everything about her was a cliché, right down to the red tip of

30

her pudgy little nose. Perhaps she wasn't actually a slob, but fat she certainly was, and thick.

'Why are you crying, Tracy?'

''Cos . . . 'cos I thought you'd be mad at me.'

'No way. You're helping us.'

'I don't know.'

'You are. Promise. Tell me again, right from the beginning.'

She sniffed, wiped her hand across the slab of her face in the general direction of her nose, frowned. Another cliché. Brow furrowed in painful concentration. Why do pretty girls – and from all the evidence, verbal and photographic, Leni Mitchell was a very pretty girl – always seem to pal up with the plain ones? Was it really only a matter of competition? Riley suspected some kind of sinister power struggle – a crudely sado-masochistic relationship, perhaps?

'Well . . . '

'Yes, Tracy. Go on.'

'Right from the beginning, do you mean, like I told you the first time or just what I said this morning?'

'From the beginning. The first time. Please.'

'All right.' She sat in silence, staring into space.

'Go on, then.'

'Aren't you going to write it down?'

'We've already written it down, Tracy . . . '

'Why do you want me to tell it all again, then?'

Riley's heart, uncharacteristically, went out to the poor clowns who had to teach her. French grammar, the themes of *A Midsummer Night's Dream* – what chance did such educational niceties stand against the thickness of Tracy Vorlander's skull? He took his pen out, uncapped it slowly, right under her eyes.

'Just to make sure we've got it down right. And if we haven't, I'll alter it as we go along. All right?'

'Yeah. If you say so.' She looked away, indifferent, tugged at her hair, sighed.

'When you are ready then, Tracy.' And to think, once, long ago, he'd actually thought of becoming a teacher.

'Well, that morning at break . . . ' Riley clamped his mouth shut. If he tried to stop her, verify dates and times, they'd be here all day. He'd just have to take the details on trust. ' . . . she says to me she says, "Hey, Trace, cover for us in H.E. this morning, will you? I'm going to bunk off for a bit." So I goes, "Why? Where you going, then?" And she goes, "Tell you later. It's a secret." So I says, "Oh, go on," but she won't. So I goes, "Well, what if old . . . Mrs Potter says anything?" And Leni goes, "Oh, she won't," but I goes, "But what if she do?" and Leni says to tell her she was feeling sick at break. So I goes, "OK." ' She must be, Riley thought bitterly, a gift to the drama department. 'So, anyway, when the bell goes she goes off to the toilet, like, and I never seen her again.' Here, as if by clockwork, tears started. Riley closed his eyes, listened to the snuffles, the blowing of the nose. 'Sorry. It's just that she was my best friend.' His eyes snapped open at the past tense but saw there was no future in questioning it. He nodded encouragingly. 'Then old . . . Mrs Potter, she spots Leni ain't there eventually. "Anyone seen Leni Mitchell?" she goes and we all go, "No, miss." Then she picks on me 'cos I'm Leni's best friend, like, and she asks me and I goes, "She was feeling a bit sick at break, miss. Perhaps she went home." And she goes, "And perhaps she's skulking in the toilets. Go and see. And if she's not there, go and ask Nurse if she reported sick. And then come straight back here." So I went.' Tracy Vorlander paused, bunched her handkerchief and sighed heavily.

'And did you look in the toilets?'

'I told you.'

'But why? You knew she wasn't there.'

'To waste time. It was only about ten minutes to the bell and then what with her memory and all the cleaning up and the boys always try to bunk off so they don't have to do the washing up, I reckoned she'd forget all about Leni.'

'And you.'

'Yeah.'

And Mrs Potter did, of course, and who could blame her?

'And then?'

'Well, then, when I'd been in the toilets, I went down the

drive 'cos I thought if she'd nipped out for something, down to the shops, like, she might be on her way back and I could warn her old . . . Mrs Potter was on the warpath. See?'

'Yes. I see. And what did you see?'

'Nothing.'

'Not Leni, I know, but you saw something . . . '

'Oh, yeah. You mean him. Yes. I saw him. This really horrible man. Ooh, horrible, he was. Really . . . horrible.'

'Tell me about him.'

'Well, he was leaning on the wall opposite, looking over into the field and he was laughing. All by himself, just laughing. And then he sort of stopped laughing and he went off down the road, ever so fast, like he was running away.'

'You didn't see anyone else at all?'

'No.'

'Tell me what you remember about the man.'

'He was horrible.'

'How horrible?'

'Ever so horrible.'

'No, I mean . . . In what way was he horrible?'

'Funny, like.'

'Funny ha-ha or . . . ?'

'No. Peculiar. He was all sort of old and dressed funny with these horrible staring eyes. Oh, it makes me scared just to think about him.'

'Yes, yes, I know. But let's try to be a bit more precise, shall we? Now, look at me, Tracy. Was he as tall as me? Taller? Shorter?'

As he read the resulting description, the Superintendent had no idea what it had cost Riley, in terms of time and patience. But it sounded good, Riley thought as he listened to it, dignified by the Superintendent's orotund tones. It sounded accurate.

' . . ."a woolly blue hat". What sort of hat would that be, Inspector?'

'Well . . . a . . . knitted hat, sir. You know the sort of thing.'

'Indeed I do, and if I'm not very much mistaken, the twenty-fifth was a very warm day, one of the best this year.'

'Absolutely, sir.'

'Not many people, I would think, were similarly coiffed that day . . . '

'Quite so, sir. He should be easy to trace. People are likely to have noticed the hat, if nothing else.'

'Is that what you want to go public on, then?'

'Yes, sir. And somebody must have seen the girl, too. I'd like to try and reconstruct a route from sightings—'

'This description's not that detailed, you know. Have you tried a Photo-fit?'

'Er, yes, sir.' Riley had been hoping to avoid this question head on.

'And?' The Superintendent prompted sharply.

'Tracy Vorlander doesn't seem able to grasp the principle, sir. She's very good on clothes, you know how fashion conscious kids are these days, but when it comes to features—'

'Surely she could get his "funny, staring eyes"?'

'She chose glasses, sir.'

'There's no mention here of glasses . . . '

'Exactly, sir.'

The Superintendent pursed his lips, tapped the report lightly with his finger.

'Perhaps she thought glasses magnified the eyes, made them appear larger?'

'I really couldn't say, sir,' Riley said, not sure if the old man was putting him on or not. 'All I know is, the whole thing was a wash-out, sir.'

'Then try an artist's impression. The girl must respond to that, surely. And, yes, you may go public with the verbal, but do try not to be alarmist. We don't have any reason to believe that she is more than a missing person.'

'No, sir. I'll tread carefully. Thank you, sir.'

Riley grabbed the report and hurried for the door.

'There is just one thing . . . '

'Yes, sir?' Riley tried, but failed, to keep the impatience out of his tone.

'I still don't understand why little Miss Vorlander didn't tell you about the man at once.'

'I honestly think she'd forgotten all about him, sir. She was scared. She's not a very bright girl, sir, with all due respect, and she was concentrating all her efforts on not dropping her friend in it.'

'In *it*?'

'Trouble, sir.'

'Ah . . . trouble . . . I see. Very well, Inspector.'

THREE

Robert could hear the women's voices, monotonous as birdsong. He stood quietly in the hall, mouthing to the accompaniment of their voices: yabber, yabber. Then, on exaggerated tiptoe, he crept to the back of the house, very, very gently opened the door of his mother's bedroom. It was a nice room, pink. He liked the way the white paint on the skirting board and window frame was all shiny and very clean. The window was open and the scent of roses, honeysuckle pervaded the room. He liked the triple mirror that showed you three people instead of one and best of all he liked the pink quilted bedhead, its satin-like sheen.

Robert stood still, concentrated. It wasn't that Mam minded him looking at them, it was just that she was afraid he would damage them in some way, so she always stood over him, fussing, and that spoiled it. It was best alone. Robert fixed his eye on the teak-veneer bedside stand. It comprised a single drawer and a cupboard with two shelves. On top was a lace doily on which stood, turned slightly towards the bed and the window, a photograph in a silver frame. Approaching the stand, Robert dropped to his knees, one of which cracked loudly. He held his breath, afraid that the sound would disturb the women, attract attention to him. He waited a long time in an attitude, almost, of prayer, then had to let his breath out in a noisy rush. Reaching up, he grasped the picture in both hands and lifted it, with great and studied care, and placed it on the bed.

It was a formal, studio portrait, taken a long time ago. Robert could sometimes just remember it. It showed his dad and mam and little Robert standing between them. Mam's hair wasn't grey then and was rolled up like a fat sausage all round her head. He did not look at his father's face. Indeed the

36

picture itself held little interest for him. He moved it because he knew he was clumsy and because it was Mam's Most Treasured Possession. Also because if he did get clumsy and knocked it over, the noise would bring the women running.

Lips twisted in concentration, he inched the drawer open. There were bottles of tablets and a packet of throat lozenges, a paperback book called *100 Popular Prayers*. And, most important of all, there was a buff-coloured folder which, gently, he lifted out and placed on the floor before him, banging his head as he stooped against the open drawer. The pills rattled. The blow hurt him but he bit his lip against the sound that wanted to come out. He pushed the drawer in a little and rubbed his forehead. Then he opened the folder and, with a surge of intense pleasure, read his name. Robert Godfrey Luman.

She had kept them all, in date order, the whole of his life up until the time of the accident. Over the years Robert's eye had become selective. Much of what was written did not interest him at all. He knew by instinct and practice which of the white, now slightly yellowing sheets held treasures and where in the narrow paragraphs of different handwritings they were hidden. *Robert is well behaved and polite, always attentive in class. Robert has made good progress this year. Robert has worked hard . . . Robert's written work is much improved . . . Well done, Robert!* He read that one twice, savoured it like a summer fruit bursting on his tongue. *Robert shows a marked aptitude for how things work and is keen to learn. A most satisfactory pupil.*

Robert leaned back, basked in a glow of pleasure and self-fulfilment. Then he narrowed his eyes and scanned the page before him so that only one word, repeated over and over, leapt out at him. *Robert. Robert. Robert.* He hugged his arms around himself and rocked gently back and forth to the rhythm of the so often repeated word: *Robert.*

The three women sat in a semi-circle, in what had become 'their' individual seats. Paula Brownlow, with her silky blonde chignon, in the solid armchair which matched the sofa where

37

Meg Sowers sat neatly, with her knees pressed firmly together. Phyllis was in her own more modern 'fireside', which had replaced the twin to Paula's chair, reducing the three-piece suite to two, a remark which never failed to make Robert laugh. All three women held work in their hands or on their laps. Paula crocheted, a delicate cotton web which grew rapidly. Meg embroidered, a piece of good linen stretched in a circular tortoiseshell frame, a patchwork bag of delicate-coloured silks beside her. Phyllis knitted, an orange Aran, the colour of which had caused much debate and some dissension between the three of them. Indeed, Paula still eyed it with a sort of malevolent disgust. Robert, however, thought it 'great' and consequently there had never been any real question of changing it, as Paula had urged. Robert liked it and therefore Robert should have it. His pleasure was more important to Phyllis than its suitability.

'Orange? On a grown man? Never!' Paula had said.

'It's very bright. It'll be cheerful on dull winter days,' Meg, as ever, had temporised.

Phyllis was realistic and unsentimental about her friends. She knew their good and bad qualities and thrived on the contrast between them. She knew, too, that without her they would not have been friends. She held them together and the knowledge that she did so gave her considerable pleasure.

Meg Sowers was too good. She knew that. She had what is inadequately known as 'a nice nature', an instinct to seek and see the good in everybody, each situation. This quality, in her, was not marred as it often is by a species of piousness. Phyllis truly thought that Meg did not turn a blind eye to that which displeased or hurt her. She had the ability to bring out what was good and positive in others because she knew no other way.

Paula was a fast-talker, an instinctive critic, the possessor of a frank and sometimes brutal tongue. She was a restless, uncomfortable woman but Phyllis had never found the cause of this. For want of other explanations, she had come to assume that, as with Meg, it was her nature to be so. She saw flaws and holes, dangers and treachery as surely as Meg noticed the warmth of a smile or an accidental act of kindness. She was a woman of judgement and rules, knew her own mind and, Phyllis thought, if it were possible to draw a picture of a mind, Paula's would be all angular hard edges, boxed in, contained, while Meg's would be a sort of yellow cloud, virtually formless, but somehow completely dependable.

These differences between her two friends – she almost thought of them as family – manifested themselves most, were indeed focused upon the perennial question of Robert, Phyllis's handling of him. She knew that Meg was too soft on her, too ready to support her decisions and attitudes without question, but if there was any danger in that, there was always Paula's astringent corrective to bring her down to earth. Paula, though, was too hard on the boy. Yet, to be fair, to Paula he must seem all flaws and because she cared with a kind of passion for Phyllis she sought to protect her from the consequences of indulgence, from, as she put it, 'making a rod for your own back'. Sometimes she added, 'You'll thank me one day,' not knowing that Phyllis did thank her, every day.

Phyllis accepted and acknowledged her dependence on these two women. They kept her going, kept her sane. They kept her in touch with a world that was naturally hers and could never be Robert's. They counterbalanced her devotion to Robert. They provided the tensions in her life which kept her alive.

Both women had husbands of their own, yet Phyllis thought of them, herself included, as equals: not quite spinsters, not quite widows, but something comfortably in between. Sometimes she felt, or felt she ought to feel, guilty about the time she took from their husbands but she hoped that she, having time and independence to encourage them, fulfilled them as they did her. All three were makers and collectors. They had, as it is commonly said, a lot in common.

'You're very quiet,' Paula said, her fingers pausing, her eyes pinning Phyllis like those of an interrogator. 'Something on your mind?'

'Is there, dear? I didn't notice. I was enjoying the quiet,' Meg said, putting aside her embroidery immediately, giving Phyllis her full attention.

'So was I. I sometimes think we chatter too much.'

'Nonsense,' Paula contradicted. 'Speech is what distinguishes man from animals.'

'Oh, I think animals talk. Communicate, anyway,' Meg said.

'It's not the same,' Paula reproved. 'Well, what were you brooding about?'

'I was just thinking,' Phyllis said, 'about us. How lucky we are. How lucky I am. I was thinking – it sounds silly and you'll scoff, I know, Paula – but I was thinking that I am very happy.'

'Well, so you should be, dear. That's nice.' Content, Meg picked up her embroidery again.

'I'm not scoffing, I just don't see how you can say that. You make the best of a bad lot, I'll say that for you, but happy, really happy . . . '

'Yes, really. I am. I've got everything I want.'

'You're a martyr,' Paula said. 'And that's the trouble with martyrs, they get to like it. I don't hold with that.'

'Oh, Paula,' Meg said quietly.

'Oh, I know how you feel about martyrs and saints. You believe what you're told, and that's all very well, but I've got to speak my mind and I say it's unhealthy.'

Words like 'unhealthy' in Paula's mouth invariably led to a discussion of Robert and that afternoon Phyllis did not want anything to tinge or colour her sense of contented well-being. An essential part of her happiness was Robert, her care for him. She put aside her knitting and stood up.

'Time for a cup of tea,' she said.

'Oh, yes. And let's put the TV on. It's nearly time for the news.'

'Why bother?' Paula said, leaning from her chair to switch on the set. 'You know it only upsets you.'

'But we have to keep informed, dear. It's best.'

Paula sighed heavily, inferring that Meg was beyond hope. Phyllis, smiling, went to make tea and while waiting for the kettle to boil went to call Robert, to see if he would take a cup of tea with them. He was in his room, lying on the bed, his nose in a Marvel comic. His room was a testimonial to her indulgence (Paula), to her attempts to provide his life with some richness (Meg) but perhaps most of all to his own restlessness. All boys had enthusiasms, grand passions that petered out as quickly as they had begun and for even less reason. The only difference was that Robert would never achieve anything to speak of just as he would never grow out of or beyond this stage. The pop phase, symbolised by the guitar and amplifier had been very noisy and not at all tuneful. Tennis had been a chore because of the lack of nearby courts. The 'running' had been quite successful and good for him, except that he sometimes got lost. Because of his leg, it wasn't really running, more a kind of strenuous walking. But it had kept him amused for a while. Phyllis smiled and bent to pick up a half-finished plastic model of . . . She could not tell whether it was a plane or a car. Yes, she did indulge him, and she made no apology for the fact. It was the least she could do.

After the accident, Phyllis seemed to spend her life at the hospital, in a world as unreal and uncertain in its own way as was Robert's. At first there had been doubt that he would live, then doubts about the nature of that life. As soon as Phyllis had a realistic idea of how her son would be, the extent of the damage, she set about providing for him. Fortunately, Daniel Luman had been well and fully insured. She decided to sell the business and the property that went with it and had stuck out for the best price she could get. She demanded and eventually got compensation for Robert. With an eye to the future, she settled on a bungalow. Prompted by instinct, she decided to move away from all that could remind Robert of the time before the accident, but her own roots and conservatism would not permit her to move away entirely. She chose the village because of the bungalow. It was far enough away from Passington, close enough to Anderton and the small town of Oversleigh to be convenient. And, yes, she did move from the city because she thought people would be kinder to and more lenient towards Robert in a small community. In that she had not been disappointed. He was an accepted part of the village.

People watched out for him, like Ken Cartwright the other day. Phyllis still did not quite understand what Robert had been doing in Oversleigh that day, walking home. His account of his adventures was a hopeless jumble. With hindsight, she saw that it was one of his bad days, definitely not the sort of day to pack him off on his own, but she had promised and he had been so looking forward to it. Besides, it did him so much good to manage for and by himself, to be a little independent now and again. And he had managed, whatever muddles there may have been or remained in his mind.

'Coming to have a cup of tea with us, Robert?'

He made one of those strange, inarticulate noises that he sometimes substituted for speech, which, at one time, in the hospital, had seemed to be all his speech. Phyllis discouraged these sounds.

'What did you say, dear? Speak properly, please.'

Robert giggled a little, stared at her.

'Don't know,' he said at last.

'Well, I shall pour you one, anyway, and take it in. If you want it, come and get it.'

'She there?'

'Who?'

'You know.'

'Then you say.'

'Paula.'

'Yes, Paula is there. And Auntie Meg.' She knew he did not like Paula, thought that he was probably afraid of her, but she drew the line at indulging him in his dislike. He and Paula rubbed along, anyway. They had to. Phyllis needed them both.

'Hello, dear. And how's Robert today? Come and sit by Auntie Meg, there's a good boy.'

'Don't treat him like a child, Meg. He's a grown man, aren't you, Robert?'

Robert stuck out his tongue at Paula, sat beside Meg who patted his hand.

'I'm sorry, Paula. Robert, that's very rude. Please don't

42

do it again.' Phyllis passed tea cups to her friends.

'That's what comes of treating him as a child. He behaves like one.'

'Shush. Here comes the news.'

Robert, who generally loved television, did not like the news. Clutching the mug his mother had given him, he stared at the back of Paula's head and wondered why her hair folded round like that. He began to tap his feet on the floor.

'Oh dear,' Meg said, her eyes glued to tragedy on the screen.

'Please, Robert,' Paula said.

'What?'

She flapped her hand at him. Meg gently placed a hand on his right knee and stilled him. Suddenly, all three women became animated, exclaiming and leaning towards the screen. Robert looked at them impatiently.

'What?' he said, and louder, 'What?'

'Quiet, Robert,' Phyllis said automatically.

Paula leaned forward and increased the volume.

' . . . *concern for the whereabouts of sixteen-year-old Lenora Mitchell who has not been seen since she left her school on Wednesday . . . '*

'Oh no,' said Meg. 'How dreadful.'

'What? What?'

'For goodness sake, Robert, shut up.'

' . . . *Inspector Riley of the Passington Police talked to reporter Paul Rebuck of EMT.'*

'*Basically, at this moment in time,*' Riley said, tugging at his tie, '*we want to appeal to anyone who may have seen Lenora since eleven twenty-five a.m. on the twenty-fifth. And, of course, if Lenora herself sees this, we urge her, please, to get in touch, either with us or her family.*'

'*Do you suspect foul play at all, Inspector?*'

'Foul, Ref. Foul. Red Card. Red Card.'

'Ssh, darling. Mummy and Auntie Paula are listening to the telly. Be a good boy.'

'I'm not anyone's Auntie Paula.'

'Why? Why? Why?'

'Because it's local, dear. See? That gentleman's speaking from Passington.'

'Been there,' Robert said proudly.

'Quiet, Robert. Just a minute,' Phyllis said.

'Drink your nice tea, dear.'

' . . . *a man we are anxious to trace, if only to eliminate him from our enquiries. Aged between thirty and forty, with protuberant eyes. He was seen in the vicinity of the school at about the time Lenora Mitchell disappeared. One very distinctive thing about him was his clothing. It was a very warm day on Wednesday and the man was dressed in a bomber-type jacket, with lots of zip pockets, grey or perhaps off-white, brown heavy-weight trousers, possibly corduroys and a knitted blue hat . . . '*

'Good God,' Paula said and twisted in her chair to stare at Robert. He looked back at her, his lower face masked by his mug. She went on staring. His mother turned to look, too, and something bad happened on her face. She stood up quickly and put the television off. Robert blew into his tea, making it bubble.

'Paula,' Phyllis said. It was a warning.

'Don't do that, dear,' Meg said. Her face was pale, with anxious little lines on it as she gently but firmly made him lower his mug.

Paula, shifting uncomfortably in her chair, glanced at Phyllis but said nothing more. The silence in the room was heavy, seemed to press in on Robert.

'What?' he demanded. 'What?'

'It's nothing, dear. It's all right,' Meg said and then, to the women, 'How dreadful. Her poor parents must be out of their minds with worry.'

'Well, I just hope they catch him, that's all,' said Paula, rattling her cup and saucer.

'She may just have run away,' Meg said hopefully.

'And pigs might fly . . . ' Robert laughed at this, rocking himself on the sofa beside Meg. 'Mark my words, she's a goner. They'll not find her alive.'

'We don't know that, Paula,' Phyllis said, moving back to her chair, smiling nervously at Robert who suddenly, extravagently, blew her a kiss.

'Oh, how sweet,' Meg said. 'That's a good boy.'

'The trouble is,' Paula went on, 'they don't do anything to them when they catch them. Just lock them up in luxury with colour television and I don't know what, and all at our expense. It's disgusting.'

'Well, we have got rid of hanging, and though it's hard, I can't really feel that's a bad thing.'

'Who's talking about hanging? Hanging's too good for them. Hard labour, the birch. That's what they ought to get. And castration. They should all be castrated. They'd understand that all right. Because they are not men. No man worthy of the name would harm a young girl—'

'Man,' Robert said loudly, his mind connecting suddenly, remembering. 'Not a child,' he said, very seriously, to Meg. 'I'm man. A proper man. Not to . . . Not a child . . . '

'Oh, for heaven's sake, shut up, Robert,' Paula shouted suddenly. 'And take that ridiculous woolly hat off.'

After she had washed up the cups and Robert's mug, rinsed and dried them and put them away on Phyllis's neat shelves, Meg went back into the sitting room and tidied it. She hated unpleasantness of any kind. She'd have to speak to Paula, or Phyllis would. Perhaps it would be better coming from Phyllis, she thought, plumping cushions, putting the orange knitting away in Phyllis's old canvas bag with the clattering wooden handles. In secret, Meg was making her a new knitting bag, in tapestry, for Christmas. She could hear Phyllis's voice, a quiet soothing drone as she moved, almost on tiptoe about the room, smoothing an antimacassar here, straightening a runner there. Thank goodness Robert was quiet now. That awful, pitiful wailing . . . Meg did not want to think about it. For a moment she felt really cross with Paula, but then, of course, it was a difficult time for Paula, her age . . . Meg thought that, possibly, childless women had a harder time of it at the change than those like her, who had been blessed with children. It seemed logical.

After all, there must be something wrong with a woman's internal workings for her to be barren, therefore it followed, surely . . . She heard Robert's door close and felt foolish suddenly, standing there daydreaming, doing nothing. She snatched up her embroidery bag and clutched it to her, as though she was just about to leave.

'You needn't have stayed, Meg, but thank you.'

Phyllis, Meg thought, had aged ten years in that last fifteen minutes; her face was pinched and drawn and there were deep, bruise-like marks under her eyes.

'I washed up and tidied . . . '

'Thank you.'

'Is all well now?'

'Yes.' Phyllis sighed. 'Have a glass of sherry, Meg. I need one.'

'Oh, no thank you, dear, no. It's a bit soon for me. But I'll gladly . . . '

'It's all right.' Phyllis wanted to say, 'Don't fuss,' but knew that would hurt Meg. She poured herself a sherry. 'Won't John be wondering where you are?' she said, not because she wanted to get rid of Meg but because she knew that she would not feel able to leave until invited, reassured.

'No. He's got an NFU meeting tonight. He won't be back until after eight and I've got supper ready . . . ' Her voice tailed away and she stood nervously, watching Phyllis sip her drink. 'Phyll, dear,' she said at last, 'you don't drink alone, do you?'

Phyllis chuckled.

'Yes, dear, I do, sometimes. But not in the way you mean. I promise.'

'That's all right, then. You didn't mind my asking?'

'Of course not.'

They were silent. Phyllis resisted the urge to knock the sherry back in one, pour herself another. Suddenly they spoke together, their voices clashing.

'I hope you won't be . . . '

'I wonder if Paula . . . '

Meg laughed less easily than Phyllis.

46

'Sorry . . . '

'Go on . . . '

'No, you. I'm sure you started first.'

'I was just going to say, I hope Paula wasn't too upset.'

'Oh, you know Paula. Her bark's worse than her bite. She'll feel thoroughly ashamed of herself and ring you up and apologise. I only hope she didn't upset *you* too much.'

'Not me,' Phyllis said sadly. 'Poor Robert . . . '

'Yes. But don't think badly of her . . . '

'I don't. You know I don't. I honestly don't know what we'd do without Paula's little outbursts. They gee us up a bit.'

'Oh, well, that's all right, then. Now I must love and leave you.'

As Meg bent to kiss her cheek and squeeze her hand, loud music, squealing guitars and amplified drums sounded from Robert's room. The women smiled at each other, knowing this meant that Robert had recovered, too. Probably he had already forgotten all about it, but it would, Phyllis knew, reinforce his dislike of Paula. Such incidents left scars. The scar tissue built up, became a constant hurt. If only she could make Paula see that.

Alone, the music making the house buzz and throb, Phyllis Luman poured herself another sherry and carried it, via the kitchen into the back garden. It was only a small plot, ending in an old-fashioned split fence which gave onto glebe land, the spire of the village church rising in the distance. She had no immediate neighbours to be disturbed by the music and it did not bother her. The incident about the hat already seemed silly. Paula, of course, should have known better. Perhaps she had genuinely forgotten. That hat was so much a part of Robert now that it had become unremarkable, unnoticeable even, unless something happened to trigger a new awareness of it.

Apart from the limp, which really did get better all the time, Robert bore only one physical scar from the accident. For some reason, the deep indentation on the left side of his head, where the cranium had been stoved in, had never grown hair again, or only a kind of fluff which fell out before it could be called hair.

When the bandages finally came off, revealing other livid scars, deliberately caused, a doctor had suggested a woolly hat and Robert had been delighted with the idea. It had become a fetish with him, a sort of comforter. Now, even Phyllis did not see him without his hat. When she wanted to wash it, she had to leave a clean one beside his bed and he would dutifully place the soiled one in the bathroom linen basket. Similarly, when she had to remind him to wash his hair, he did so in the strictest privacy, the bathroom door locked, a blind drawn down over the frosted window. And he stayed in there until his hair was dry and the hat could be replaced. Each year, Phyllis knitted him a new hat, sometimes two. Always blue. They reminded her of sad bluebells as they dangled limply from her four needles. They were her son's protection and, in a funny way, perhaps his vanity. Paula should have known better.

It was the sort of mistake, of course, caused by shock and irritation, growing in the atmosphere of closeness caused by seeing somewhere familiar on a television screen, that anyone could make. In all probability there never was any such man. People, in Phyllis's view, were often notoriously eager and imaginative to spot the sinister loiterer when something terrible appeared to have happened on their own, no-longer-safe doorsteps. But if he did exist he had probably already presented himself at Passington police station to prove his innocence. A workman, probably. A bald man, most likely, protecting his head from the sun. Bald men burned and peeled so easily, she thought, probably because their skin was tender, being designed to be protected by a layer of hair. That was it, almost certainly. It was foolish of her even to consider . . . Unworthy, even.

Going back into the house with thoughts of supper darting in her mind, Phyllis was greeted by silence and, slightly disturbed by this because once Robert fixed on his record collection he usually played it right through, for hours on end, she went into the hall, to the door of his room. As she was about to knock, her eye was caught by his jacket, hanging on the peg just inside the front door. It was neither grey nor off-white, more a sort of cream or beige. And there was nothing unusual or distinctive about it. Robert had chosen it from a rail of dozens similar, from a chain store. The many glittering zips had attracted him and she had seen their usefulness since Robert was apt to lose things. But she lifted the jacket down and held it against her as she knocked and called.

'Are you all right, Robert?'

'Yeah.'

'Not playing your records?'

'No.'

'I'm going to get supper soon. What are you doing?'

'Reading.'

'All right, dear.' She turned away from the door, saw that she was still holding the jacket. She turned back. 'I'm going to wash your jacket, Robert. Better put your other one out for tomorrow.' He did not reply. She carried the jacket into the kitchen and placed it in the scarlet plastic basket on top of the washing machine, then opened the refrigerator and took out a packet of sausages, the basis of Robert's supper.

Ever since the accident, the only true consistency in Robert's mental life, secret and unarticulated, had been a desire, burning, urgent, to be someone, to be famous, to be again the boy of promise who lived for him now in the prison of yellowing school reports. Therein lay the root of his passions, his enthusiasms. His room, though no one perceived it as such, perhaps least of all Robert, was a museum of and memorial to his frustration, a dead place, without hope. Currently, he wanted to be Superman or the Silver Surfer or Spiderman, a legendary hero whose image and adventures he devoured day after day from the pile of comic books that stood beside his bed. He had discovered this new, childishly masculine world last year when, at the village fête, his eye had lit upon a pile of comics, neatly tied with string, on the nearly-new stall. Since then he had added to his collection, scanning the newsagents of Oversleigh and Anderton at every opportunity. His appetite for them was unquenchable, their pictures and idiosyncratic vocabulary sheer magic.

Robert was growing more like Superman every day. When his mother knocked on the door that evening, he was engrossed in verifying this fact. His records were old, stale and boring. Nowhere, ever, had he known Superman or any other hero to listen to music. Stripped to the waist, he stood before his mirror, bunching his shoulders, knotting his muscles, seeing in the reflection the two-dimensional curves and bulges that proclaimed the hero's strength. If his eye ever showed him any disparity between his physique and that of Superman, he knew it was temporary, would be instantly remedied by the right clothing, the uniform of legend. But mostly he saw only similarities, a growing oneness between himself and the image. More than anything in the world, Robert wanted a Superman costume, complete and exact down to the last detail. If he asked Mam, if he asked her nicely . . . Hurrying to pull on his shirt, Robert caught sight of his blue hat in the mirror. It was a little askew, disturbed by his hurried undressing and dressing. He put it straight. He remembered that bad look on Mam's face. He did not understand why, did not understand at all why she had looked at him like that, why Mam had been afraid. He hated Paula Brownlow, hoped she'd slip and break her big fat leg. Hoped she'd die. Going on at him. Going on at him. Shouting. All because of his hat. When he got his Superman costume he'd . . . With a terrible feeling of pain and disappointment, of black hopelessness, Robert remembered that Superman did not wear a hat. And, in a moment of rare but cruel clarity, he saw that his blue hat, his habitual and necessary blue hat would look stupid with a Superman costume. His world crumbled. He felt himself isolated, defeated, saw himself almost as others did. Robert threw himself down on his bed and began to wail.

Early next morning, after a disturbed and restless night, Phyllis Luman began to load the washing machine. It had taken her two hours to pacify Robert last night, to draw out of him the cause of his distress. She still did not fully understand it but she knew she'd promised to make him a suit of some kind with a black hood, like one of those strange creatures in his comic books. She hoped he would forget about that, for he would not be able to wear it outside the house and Robert got so attached to clothes. She would face that one when and if she came to it, she told herself firmly. Maybe he would forget about it. It had pacified him. That was all that mattered. She had persuaded him to drink some warm milk, swallow one of his 'special' pills, the ones that calmed him by sending him into a deep sleep, the ones she hated giving him, only administered in emergencies. He would sleep late this morning, would probably feel groggy and be lethargically passive all day. She welcomed the peace that would bring her, but hated buying it chemically, at such a cost. If only she knew, really knew what went on in his mind.

As she always did with Robert's clothes, Phyllis made a systematic search of his pockets. Before she got into this habit, many garments, several whole loads of washing had been ruined and one machine all but wrecked by the alien items Robert carefully pocketed and promptly forgot. From his jacket she extracted a packet of Marlboro, half-full, some loose change, several spent matches and a sticky boiled sweet, some softened sticks of gum. The outside breast pocket with its slanting, angled zipper, seemed empty, felt flat, but she had learned that touch alone could be deceptive. She undid it and fished inside with two fingers, pulling out a pink bus ticket. She was about to throw it away when its colour held her attention. She brought it close to her eyes, tilted it towards the light: *Return. Passington. £1.80.* And the truncated date: *25.6.*

She was still holding the ticket minutes later, her mind racing, refusing, denying, when she heard Paula let herself in, calling from the hallway. She stuffed the jacket into the washing machine, turned quickly towards the pedal bin, the ticket still clutched in her fingers, but somehow could not, dare not, throw it away.

'In the kitchen,' she called.

She saw the dustmen emptying the bins, the scrap of pink paper caught in a breeze, blown down the street, growing larger and more sinister . . . Turning guiltily to greet Paula, she slipped the ticket into the pocket of her skirt.

'Phyll, Phyll, I'm so sorry. What can I say? I never slept a wink. Look, I've brought these for Robert. I hope he hasn't got them . . . '

Wondering, pleased but still scared, Phyllis took the brightly coloured comics from Paula's outstretched hands.

'But where on earth did you . . . ?'

'I got up early and drove straight into Oversleigh. Raided every newsagent in town. Please say you forgive me . . . ?'

'Oh, don't be so silly. There's no need . . . This is very kind, Paula. He'll be so pleased.' Phyllis put the comics down on the kitchen table.

'Oh yes there is and you must let me say one thing . . .'

'Please, Paula . . . '

'You look dreadful. Are you all right?'

'I'm fine. Just a bit tired. I didn't have a very good night . . . '

'Sit down. Go on. I'll make you a cup of tea. Shall I start the washer for you?'

'No. Leave it.' The chair that she dragged from the table felt like it was made of lead. She sank weakly into it. Paula spoke above the rattle of the kettle, the rush of water.

'What I wanted to say was, you must believe me, I didn't even think it . . . you know? . . . About the hat, I mean. It was just coincidence. I never even . . . I swear to you, Phyll, I never even thought it.'

'I know, Paula. I know. Don't worry about it, please.'

Beneath the table, out of sight, Phyllis put her hand protectively over the bus ticket where it lay in her pocket, against her thigh. It seemed to burn through the lining of the pocket, into her flesh.

'So I really am forgiven, then?'

'Of course, dear. I know it was nothing. I know it's all a stupid mistake.'

FOUR

Karen Ashburton watched her lover of two months moving around the room, packing a notebook, pen and pencils, a flat manila folder into a briefcase she had not seen before. He wore the trousers of a dark suit, a little too tight for him, slightly old-fashioned and with the sort of crease that only comes from recent, professional cleaning. With it a white shirt and plain, yellow wool tie. The jacket of the suit hung, still sheathed in flimsy plastic, on the back of the door. He closed the briefcase with a double 'snap' and came to the bed, leaned over, looked at her. His smartness made him seem alien, while the neatness of his hair, his well-scrubbed, groomed look and the smell of his aftershave made Karen feel tacky and unclean.

'You awake, love?'

'Yeah.' She turned her head a little away from him, focused on the jacket in its plastic caul. 'You're a bit over the top, aren't you?' she said, not meaning it to sound quite so grumpy and accusing.

'Got to make a good impression,' he said lightly, settling himself beside her. She moved across the bed, essentially to make room for him but it felt, to both of them, like a withdrawal. He sighed. 'It's important to me. It'll make all the difference if I get this.'

'I know.'

She knew. It would mean that he would move away and nothing had been said about her, where she would fit in. Besides, she did not believe the job – head of the art department at Breeton College was right for him. She thought that he was walking into a bigger trap than the one he had recently escaped. Instead of lumbering himself with more responsibilities and commitments, which would eat into his time and sap his energies, Karen wanted him to develop his own

53

work, paint, get a show together . . . The fact that she could see herself fitting into that life pattern was a bonus, not the *raison d'être*.

'Aren't you going to wish me luck?'

'Yes, of course.' She sat up suddenly, flung her arms around him, held him, smelt him with a passion that frightened both of them. He held her lightly with one arm, stroked her thick, naturally curling hair with the other hand.

'And you will remember, ten sharp? Please. They're sticklers for punctuality.'

'I bet they are,' Karen said coldly, releasing him and flopping back on the bed, covering her breasts with the sheet. Tom stood up, fussing with the creases in his trousers.

'Look, if you're not going to do it, just say so and I'll . . . '

'I'll do it. I said I would.'

'And I've said I'm sorry. I shouldn't have volunteered you. I won't do it again.'

'Don't worry. I won't be any good, anyway . . . '

'You'll be great.'

She didn't care one way or the other. More than her doubts about the job, the whole direction he was letting circumstances force him into, she had been appalled at the 'little favour' he had asked of her. She hadn't even known that, from time to time, he worked for the police, making artist's impressions of missing people and wanted men when no suitable photograph existed or those clumsy, biased Photo-fits didn't work for some reason. She hated the idea of helping the police. The mere idea of doing so felt like a betrayal of everything she stood for. To her it was worse than a straightforward commercial prostitution of such talents as she had. She could forgive him doing such work. It was just another example of the way Marie, his about-to-be ex-wife had ground him down and pigeon-holed him. Just as this job he was after, for all his fine arguments about career prospects and security was just so that he could pay Marie top-whack alimony and indulge – no, pay for – her snobbish ideas about how their kids should be educated. It was all part of that same, awful treadmill that Karen knew squeezed the creativity

54

out of him. If she didn't do something now, he would be a dried-up husk by the time he was forty.

All this and more Karen had said last night but somehow she had ended up agreeing to stand in for him at the police station, and now she had wished him luck with the interview.

'Ask for DI Riley, remember,' he said, buttoning his jacket.

'OK. Yes. Old Mother Riley.'

'You're impossible.'

'I hate it.'

'Please don't let's start that again.' He looked impatiently at his watch, picked up the briefcase, symbol of all she feared for him. 'Well . . . '

'What's the matter with your old satchel?' Karen asked, pushing one foot out of the bed and nudging the case.

'Not likely to impress the principal and his governors.'

'But if you get the job, you'll use it, every day. Besides, I love that old satchel . . . '

'Karen, you're such a kid . . . '

'Then you're a hypocrite . . . ' She saw his mouth tighten under the glossy black moustache that made him look a little like the young Clark Gable and yet gave him an air of distinction. 'No, you're not,' she corrected herself quickly, seeking his thigh with her toes. 'It's just the rotten awful bloody system.'

'Well, you take the whole police force on and I'll jump through a few more hoops and may the best person win, OK?'

'Don't patronise me . . . '

'I'm not. Just teasing.' He bent over her and she threw her arms around his neck, pulling him down, kissing him.

When he pulled away, patting smooth the hair on the back of his head, she said: 'When will you be back?'

'I don't know. Ring me.'

'All right. And I hope you get it if you really want it.'

'Thank you.'

She crossed her fingers under the bedclothes and hoped that he would not. Better he feel depressed, rejected . . . She could handle that. She could handle anything, if only . . .

'Right, then . . . '

'If you say "ten o'clock sharp" again, I swear I won't go.'

He grinned.

'I was going to say I love you.'

'I love you too.'

It was true, Karen thought, snuggling down, waiting to hear his car start. She loved him and she loved that scuffed old satchel, which flopped now empty, despised, on the seat of a chair. The satchel was one of the first things she had noticed about him when she had gone to the tech and met Thomas J. Skidmore, head of the foundation year. It was the sort of satchel you still saw occasionally looped over the shoulders of small boys going to posh private schools, bouncing on the small of their backs as they hurried to catch the gleaming minibus or to their parents' affluent cars. Tom wore his, ink- and paint-stained over one shoulder, the flap invariably flapping open. It made him look artistic, she thought, that and his tight jeans, red leather boots and brightly coloured shirts. It seemed now that she had fancied him from the very first, though this wasn't strictly speaking true. But the satchel had marked him out as different, a sensitive man, still in touch with his childhood, which was something that appealed and was important to Karen. She had not found growing up particularly hard and had certainly embraced the advantages of adulthood with enthusiastically opened arms, but it scared and mystified her the way 'grown-ups', as she still privately thought of them, seemed to cut themselves off from their childhoods, took up a stance towards children that seemed to say, I was never like that, boisterous, noisy, above all, happy. She did not understand why those of her friends who had children found them such a nuisance. She thought that kids were great and rested her case.

But there was a conventional and possibly sensible part of her that was glad that Tom Skidmore had not crossed that invisible line between staff and students until Marie had left him. She had enjoyed fancying him in the vague, expectation-free way she had fancied the young gym master at the boys' high when she was fourteen. Tom had become real and adult for her at a student party, to which he had only been invited because he was considered to be 'all right' and lonely and miserable because his marriage had broken up. Sharing a joint with him, Karen had seen him anew, had seen the lost look in his eyes as temporary disorientation, like that of a caged animal newly returned to the wild. She had seen his potential and the little boy in him and now she had fallen in love with him.

Karen was no fool. Getting out of bed, forcing herself to go through the morning routine of washing and brushing her teeth, she admitted that she was out of her depth and that she was scared and that it was marvellous. She had been in love many times before, to the consternation and anger of all the 'grown-ups' around her, but she had never been this deeply involved. Part of her could even wish that she was not. She hated the instinct to insinuate herself into Tom's future. She wanted to give him what she knew was right for him without considering herself, her own fate, but every time she argued that he needed more time to paint, to see himself as an artist and only as a part-time teacher and administrator, she saw herself by his side. She knew that she could not be the lover of the head of art at Breeton College. Oh, she could take it on somehow – she was no stranger to compromise – but she knew that she would not fit. There was no place for her there. She knew, with a feeling of dread, that if it came to that, she would become an embarrass-ment to Tom, a career hamper. Well, that's what she wanted to be, *vis-à-vis* Tom, she told the mirror defiantly, making her scalp tingle with hard, swift strokes of the hairbrush. She wanted to be a student, taking odd, menial jobs to scrape a bit of money together. She wanted to be an artist surrounded by other artists. She wanted to inspire and create, be dependent and independent. The only trouble was, she could no longer imagine doing any of it without Tom.

Riley stared at her, as did the other, uniformed men behind the counter, though all but the youngest had the grace to shuffle papers, make some pretence of busyness.

She was a tall, lanky girl – nothing to her, Riley thought – in crumpled black trousers and a shocking pink jacket on which the CND badge glowed like a declaration of war. She had sharp, pointed features, devoid of make-up, which made the long, unmatched earrings seem oddly out of place. And then the hair, which was very thick and springy and curly, which was neither red nor blonde nor dyed, was looped back on one side with a little girl's bow of pink ribbon which seemed to contradict her frowning, pugnacious manner. She carried a large sketch-pad under one arm and a child's zip-up pencil case in the other.

'Karen Ashburton?' Riley said.

'Yeah. Tom Skidmore sent me. You're supposed to be expecting me.'

'That's right,' he said, and moved to raise the counter flap for her. She stood there, nostrils flaring, as though afraid to come through, cross the line into police territory. 'You'd better come through and I'll explain the set-up.'

Heads turned to look at her as she followed Riley through some kind of communal office. Karen, head high, trying not to notice the open scrutiny, thought she despised the neat-shirted police women – all doing menial jobs, of course, bashing typewriters and making coffee and filing cards – more than the men, though at least the girls looked pallid and indifferent, while the men, secure in their tyrannous space, made no effort to conceal what they thought of her. One even pouted his lips as though to whistle at her, but thought better of it. Another scratched his crotch. At least she thought he was scratching.

Riley led her into a little box of an office, all glass and clutter, and offhandedly told her to sit down. He remained standing, behind his desk, staring at her.

'I'm all right,' she said, sliding the pad onto the desk, toppling some papers towards him. She was damned if she was going to apologise. He stared at them. He cleared his throat.

'You've done this sort of work before?'

'No.'

'What are you, then, an artist of some kind?'

'Yes. I'm also a student at the tech. If I'm not properly qualified, I'll go.'

'Hang on a minute . . . No need to be like that . . . I was only
. . . '

'Checking?'

'Look, Tom Skidmore said you could do the job. That's good
enough for me.'

'Fine. What do I do?'

'Basically, it's a question of talking to the girl, asking her
what she remembers and seeing if you can draw something she
recognises.'

'All right.'

'She's given us a verbal description but, well, it's a bit short
on detail. I expect you'd like to see it . . . ' He leaned over the
desk, rummaging, moving papers from one muddled pile to
another.

'No, thanks.' Karen shook her head, making her hair, the
ribbon and the earrings dance. 'I'd rather start without
preconceptions. Can I talk to the girl? Ask her questions?'

'Sure. But anything you learn is confidential.'

'Naturally,' Karen said. 'Who is she? What am I supposed to
sketch?'

'A bloke she saw.' He almost added, 'Or thought she saw,'
but did not even want to think about that. It was still the only
lead they had. 'Her mate's gone missing. You've probably read
about it?' Karen shook her head again. 'As far as we know, she
was the last to see the missing girl, Lenora Mitchell. We've
done a search of the area, but nothing. So maybe this bloke she
says she saw . . . Anyway, it's our only concrete lead.'

'She must be pretty upset,' Karen said.

'Upset?'

'If her friend's missing . . . '

'Oh. Yes. I suppose. The thing is, she's not very bright, not
very verbal, you know? You'll have to be patient with her.'

Like you were, I bet, Karen thought, but only nodded.

'What's her name?'

'Tracy Vorlander.'

They stared at each other. Karen said: 'So, can I see her
now? Get started?'

'Yes. Sure.' He still stood there.

'Is something wrong?'

'No, I'll take you down . . . '

The words conjured up an image of cells, of some poor little girl, confused and intimidated. Karen knew exactly how she must feel. But first she had to run the gauntlet of the office again, the stares, the whispered comments. Then she was back in the reception area and thought, for one brief, happy moment, that Riley was going to tell her thanks, but no thanks. Instead he turned left down a blind corridor and left again.

A large woman and a large girl sat huddled silently on a bench outside a green-painted door labelled 3 in stencilled white paint.

'Mrs Vorlander,' Riley said, nodding. 'Hello, Tracy. This is . . . '

'Hello, Tracy,' Karen said, stepping forward, smiling. 'My name's Karen. I'm ever so sorry to hear about your friend. This . . . Mr Riley's been telling me all about it and I'm going to try and draw this man you saw. Is that OK with you?'

The girl's mouth worked. Slowly she lifted her rather dog-like pale eyes to meet Karen's. Mrs Vorlander nudged her, making her body sway.

'Yes, miss.'

'Call me Karen. Great. Let's see if we can get started, then.' She turned to Riley who, with a start, opened the door and stood back. 'Come on, Tracy.' She touched the girl's shoulder and slowly she stood, shuffled ahead of Karen into the room. Karen turned, looked Riley in the eyes. 'You don't have to be here, do you?'

'Well . . . '

'It'll be better if you're not.'

'I thought you were new to this?'

'I'm a quick learner,' Karen said, and smiled at him. 'I expect Mrs Vorlander'd like a cup of tea or something,' she told him and slipped into the room, closing the door firmly but gently in his face.

* * *

60

The interview room was small, its only window set so high as to be forbidding and to direct the light uselessly in a replica of itself on the ceiling and opposite wall. Karen turned on the electric light, a single bulb with a green conical shade which did little to brighten the gloom. Tracy pulled out one of the two chairs and sat as though sitting was the only comfortable posture known to her body.

'That's a lovely cardigan, Tracy,' Karen said, coming to the table. 'Where did you get it?'

'My nan knitted it.'

'She must be very clever. It's a lovely colour. You like bright colours? What do you think of my pencil case? Bright, isn't it?'

'Yes.'

'I bet they won't let you wear that to school, though, eh? You not going in today?'

'They said I could have a few days off. What with the police and everything . . . '

'Well, I bet you don't mind that too much, do you?'

'No, miss. Only it's boring at home. Nothing to do.'

'I expect you miss your friend. Lenora, is it?'

'Leni, miss. We call her Leni.'

'Oh that's a great name. I like that. And mine's Karen, remember?'

'Yes, mi . . . Karen.'

'Tell me about Leni. What's she like?' Karen opened her pad and picked out a pencil.

'She's all right. You know . . . She's a laugh. Good fun.'

'I bet you miss her then, don't you?'

'Yes, mi . . . Yes.'

'And you must be worried about her?'

'Yes.'

'Well, then, let's see what you can tell me about this man you saw.'

'I've told them, miss. Over and over.'

'But you haven't told me. Just think about him . . . Tell me anything that comes into your head. Try to . . . picture him . . .'

61

Karen waited. Tracy shifted in her chair, crossed her ankles, stared at them.

'You're not like a policeman,' she said at last, timidly.

Karen laughed. It was a good laugh, loud and robust. Tracy smiled sheepishly.

'That's because I'm not. I'm a student. An artist. I'm just doing this to help out a friend. And all I'm going to do is try to draw this man you saw, draw him as good as I can until you say, "Yeah, that's him." OK? And I'll tell you something else. I'm on your side.' The girl looked at her warily, searched her face for some sign of a lie, a trick. 'Honest.'

'They scare me,' Tracy said at last.

'They scare me, too. So let's make a start, eh? The sooner we get it done, the sooner we can get out of here.'

'All right. Well, he was really funny-looking, you know? Really sort of horrible . . . '

Karen tried again. Her head had begun to ache, a tight band pressing just above her eyes.

'Cheeks sort of sucked in,' Tracy said, chewing gum now, seated beside Karen, watching her pencil fly.

'Sunken,' Karen said, smoothing shadows onto the paper with her thumb.

'I wish I could draw.'

'You should take lessons.'

'No.'

'How's that?'

'Great.'

'Is it like him?'

'Well . . . '

Karen started again, trying to combine the bits of previous attempts that Tracy found acceptable, trying to make them fit into a coherent whole. They were interrupted by a woman police officer bringing them coffee. She said Mr Riley would like to know how much longer they were going to be. Karen said, without conviction:

'Nearly there.'

She stared at the drawing, adding unnecessary details to the hat while Tracy, her tongue loosened now, enthused about George Michael.

'The thing is, I can't make up my mind whether I like him best with or without his beard. He's so fab, dreamy . . . I got thirteen posters . . . '

Karen did not listen. As Tracy drifted deeper into her fantasy world, delivering a commentary on what would never be, Karen saw a way of connecting the disparate elements of the face she had drawn. It appealed to her now, even excited her a little, as an exercise. She forgot entirely why she was required to draw this face. The girl's slow, monotonous chatter acted like soothing background music. Her pencil moved quickly, steadily. Hunched over the drawing, she worked on details, fashioning a line here, a crease there, adjusting the lips and softening the eyes. It was purely an exercise, a rescue job, an application of technique to solve a problem. And when she finished, satisfied, she held the pad at arm's length and studied the result. Karen burst into laughter.

'What? What is it? Let's see. Come on, let's see.'

'No, it's no good. I've completely blown it.'

The girl snatched the pad, held it before her. Karen, still laughing at the trick her own subconscious had played on her, watched Tracy's face, saw it set and pale.

'Ooh, that's him. That's him, miss. You've got him perfect. Oh, you are clever.'

Karen cooled her heels for half an hour in the reception area before a red-faced constable came to fetch her. During that time she had come close to walking out at several points, only her pad and the enormity of what the picture itself must mean if she could not make them understand kept her there. She would kill Tom for getting her into this mess. She felt vindicated that she had proved that she was no good at this sort of thing. If only she could make them understand. Tracy, watched by her doughy, suspicious mother, came up to her after fifteen minutes.

'I'm sorry, miss, if I've done wrong.'

'Of course you haven't done wrong, Tracy. It's not your fault. It's all mine. I just lost my concentration.' Tracy stared at her doubtfully. 'Honestly. You've nothing to blame yourself for.' Karen glanced at the waiting woman. 'Are you off now?'

'Yes, miss.'

'Go on then. Nice meeting you, Tracy.'

'And you, miss. 'Bye.'

''Bye, Tracy.'

And then she went all over it again in her head, cursing herself for being so damn stupid, so at once inattentive and absorbed in her work. She cursed Tom and the police, her wasted morning and then, again, herself. Worst of all was the knot of fear, of dread and helplessness that had lodged in her stomach and which made her jump when the constable appeared, calling her name, holding up the flap for her. He took her not back to Riley's office, not through the crowded outer office but into a silent lift which flowed smoothly up and then along a carpeted corridor to a door with a nameplate: Superintendent E. G. Tait.

He rose as she entered the light, airy room with its fine view out over the city, the cathedral spire rising like an accusing finger. She saw Riley, dishevelled and fuming, scramble to his feet from an easy chair in the corner of the room and glare at her. Tait leaned, smiling and affable, over his meticulously neat, highly polished desk and offered his hand. Karen hated herself for noticing, as she reached out to take it, that her own hand was black with pencil markings, with dark crescents under each neat nail.

'Miss Ashburton,' Tait said, holding her little girl's dirty paw in both of his smooth, pink hands and smiling at her. 'Thank you so much for your patience and *all* your help. Mr Riley has explained that you came to us in our hour of need and, I must say, with very gratifying results. Do, please, sit.' He released her hand at last and Karen groped for the chair behind her, sat. Say something, she screamed at herself. Make him understand.

'Ashburton . . . ' Tait mused, seating himself, hitching his chair into the desk and making a tent of his clean fingers. 'You know, I do believe I know your father. Reginald Ashburton, lives at Brindsleigh? Executive with the CEGB, if I'm not mistaken. A prominent figure in the Round Table and something of an enthusiast for Gilbert and Sullivan?'

At this, Karen burst out laughing. Her father's painful cavorting with the Oversleigh Gilbert and Sullivan Society, his lustily inaccurate baritone had tortured her childhood. In spite of herself, she liked Tait, liked his confident knowledge and the slight edge to his tone, then told herself not to be so daft; he was a policeman.

'Do you sing yourself?'

'Only when I'm driving or in the bath.' She thought she heard Riley muffle a snicker at this and glared at him. He looked ostentatiously out of the window, playing with the unravelling elastic knitted into the top of his short loud blue sock.

'Well, you have other talents, remarkable ones . . . '

'Look,' Karen said, drawing her chair closer to the desk. 'That picture is a mistake. I've explained to Mr Riley. That is not the man Tracy described. The whole thing is a terrible mistake. I'm very sorry I've wasted your time but . . . '

'On the contrary . . . '

'Please, if you'll just give me the picture . . . I'm sure Tom Skidmore will be able . . . '

'Please, Miss Ashburton, do tell me why you are so convinced this is not the man Tracy Vorlander described to you.' From a drawer on his right, he drew her pad, folded open at the drawing. Upside down, the eyes seemed to accuse her or beg her.

'Right,' she said with a confidence she did not feel. Play it up, she told herself. Stress your incompetence. Let them think what they bloody well like only . . . 'As you know, I've never done this sort of thing before. I was nervous. I said to Tom, Mr Skidmore, that I didn't think I'd be any good . . . '

'But this is excellent, very fine. You do yourself an injustice, Miss Ashburton.'

'But that's just the point. It's a picture. A picture out of my head, not an impression of what Tracy saw. Look, Tracy only

65

remembers bits and pieces – the hat, his eyes . . . '

'His "staring" eyes. These are not noticeably staring, would you say?'

'No. Because . . . You see, I'd made these few attempts and all I'd got were bits and pieces, nothing that would fit into a face, even an impression of a face. She had no idea about the ears, the mouth . . . Anyway, the point is, I lost my concentration, forgot what I was supposed to be doing . . . Somebody brought us a cup of coffee and Tracy was rattling on and I just started messing around with the picture, with the elements I'd got, for my own amusement, if you like, and my . . . instinct, my memory, I suppose, just took over. I started to draw a picture . . . '

'Incorporating these very elements, though, no?'

'Yes. But altering them. Like the eyes. You noticed that yourself—'

'Only that they were not particularly protuberant . . . '

'I altered them, I tell you, and without meaning to, I drew someone else, from memory. I made a different picture, out of my head, my memory. That's a picture of someone I know.'

'You know him?' Riley was on his feet, coming towards her.

'Yes. That's the point. And he couldn't possibly have been . . . '

'What's his name? Do you know where he lives?'

'Yes.'

'Well, come on, then . . . ' Riley said, hectoring her, impatient. Karen looked from him to Tait, who studied her with an unreadably bland expression.

'I won't tell you,' Karen said.

'It's your duty to tell us. We can have you for . . . '

'That's enough, Riley, thank you,' Tait said with quiet but definite command. 'Mr Riley is naturally very anxious to solve this case, Miss Ashburton. In confidence, I can tell you we have little to go on and we fear, increasingly fear, for Lenora Mitchell's safety. This man,' he tapped the drawing with a stiff, certain finger, 'is our only substantial lead. He may be the last person to have seen the girl . . . He may have vital information . . . '

66

'And he might be a murderer,' Riley interrupted, 'and you sit there and say you won't tell us . . . '

'Thank you, Riley. Perhaps you'd care to go and . . . er . . . check some of your other lines of enquiry. I'd like to talk to Miss Ashburton alone.'

For a moment it seemed that Riley would explode, or flatly refuse, or attack Karen. All possibilities warred across his face until Tait spoke again, quietly, just his name.

'Yes, sir.'

He even managed not to slam the door as he left.

'Phew!' Karen said.

'You must understand that Mr Riley's under a great deal of pressure. We are all very concerned for this young woman.'

'I can understand that. God, I'm concerned. But it's nothing to do with . . . ' Karen bit her lip, flushed when Tait smiled at her near slip.

'Do you mind if I smoke?' Tait asked, producing a packet of small, individually wrapped cheroots. 'I assume I cannot offer you one,' he said, still smiling, when Karen nodded. 'Although young ladies these days . . . '

'No. Thanks.' He unwound the Cellophane from the dull brown leafy tube as though relishing the act. 'About the girl, Leni Mitchell. Tracy said something that might be really useful.' Even as she spoke, something inside Karen cringed. She was acting like a police informer. Why did Tom ever get her into this? But even that was better than letting them think that her picture, her bloody stupid picture . . . 'I got her confidence, I think. Got her to relax, anyway, and I slipped her the odd question, when she was off her guard, I suppose,' Karen said ruefully.

'You'd make an excellent detective then, Miss Ashburton. Such techniques are valued and practised in the force . . . '

Karen swallowed this, told herself not to be drawn, to get on with it, distract him from the picture.

'Anyway, I asked her, casually, why *she* thought Leni had walked out of school that morning. I didn't make any suggestions, give her any alternatives. Just asked her, point blank, her opinion.' Tait nodded again, watching her as he lit the little cigar. 'She said, "To see a boy, miss. I reckon she went to see a boy."'

'And were you able to discover anything about this hypothetical boy? A particular boy, was it, or just any boy, in general, so to speak?'

'No.' Karen felt defeated. 'I tried but she took off about George Michael . . . '

'She named somebody?'

'No. George Michael's a pop singer she's keen on. That's all.'

'Mr Michael is irrelevant?'

'Absolutely.'

'Well, that's very valuable information, Miss Ashburton. And you are to be congratulated. Poor Mr Riley has elicited no opinions from our little Miss Vorlander . . . A boy, you say . . . '

'It would seem likely, at that age. She's a pretty girl from the photos I've seen . . . '

'And, of course, you would know.' Karen did not know how to take this. 'I mean, being so close to that age yourself, so attractive and a woman.'

Karen said nothing. Wreaths of blue, scented, almost spicy smoke rose in the sunlight. Karen watched them. Tait watched Karen then suddenly waved his hand, dismissing the smoke.

'I can understand your distress about the picture. I can also understand, as perhaps Mr Riley cannot, how such an artistic accident could come about, but we do have one rather difficult problem.'

'Which is?'

'The Vorlander girl swears this is a true and accurate likeness. "Spot on" is, I believe, the phrase she used.'

After Superintendent Tait had escorted the confused and distressed and angry Ashburton girl to the lift, he returned to his office determined to let Riley stew in his own frustration for a while longer. He enjoyed the prospect, but that was not his motivation. He was always a pretend sadist, and then only out of expediency. He needed time to think. Everything he had learned that morning prompted him towards caution. A little diplomacy was required. For one thing, Reginald Ashburton was a valuable acquaintance, a man his instincts, if only for the sake of the Police Fund, prompted him to keep sweet. As the police force moved inevitably into the public arena of controversy, solid men like Ashburton were invaluable and Tait knew that Ashburton and most of his Round Table colleagues were waiting in the wings, ready to take up the cudgels should they be needed. He winced at his own mixture of metaphors and decided to let them stand.

Ashburton's daughter on the other hand, though a nonentity, of course, could be said to represent the potential enemy. An intelligent and verbal young woman, she could make a damaging noise and she was a fully paid up member of that hotbed of leftist dissent, the polytechnic. She had the makings of a figurehead and the rash will of the young and ill-informed. Tait did not fear her but then he did not want to stir up unnecessary ripples.

The social and political side of the matter thus neatly summarised, Tait applied his mind to the pressing business in hand. Here, oddly, he found himself veering towards Karen Ashburton's view. He believed that a picture could emerge, form itself thoughtlessly. Thoughtlessness was perhaps the accurate definition of that alarmingly vague phrase 'artistic inspiration'. He knew that the memory could offer the oddest material at the most inopportune times. He had always, of course, assumed that a boy lurked somewhere in the Mitchell mystery. People might think him out of touch but he had two grown boys of his own, had been a boy himself and his memory was vivid. But, and here was the nub of it, the indissoluble piece of grit to which his mind always and necessarily returned: unlike Riley, eager, undisciplined Riley, he did not, as Riley himself would say, 'buy' the Vorlander girl's story. If she had seen such a man as she now inadequately described, she would have said so at her first interview. In all probability she would have reported his lurking presence to a member of the school staff immediately. Young girls had lurid imaginations, were weaned on gutter-press accounts of strange men with staring eyes, who raped and slaughtered and abducted. They thrived on it, in Tait's bitter view. No, he had never been entirely convinced by Vorlander's sudden recall. Vorlander was making herself interesting, was buying time off school and getting lots of lovely attention. The boy, on the other hand, had the ring of truth about him, not the scary, funny man who had so oddly slipped her mind for upwards of twenty-four hours.

But Riley's conviction, the lack of any other material lead, despite searches and house-to-house enquiries, together with the possible evidence of the Ashburton girl's excellent artwork remained. All must be accommodated. All must be dealt with, but gently, gently, in a diplomatic fashion.

Satisfied, Tait sent for Riley and in his flattest, most uninflected tone, told him what he had decided. He enjoyed watching the rumpled man fume and admired the way he held himself – from fear? – on a tight rein. Tait explained what they would do, how to proceed. He urged Riley to scour the land if necessary for that boy, any boy, for Lenora Mitchell must have had boyfriends, surely? And he, Tait, would personally contact DS Jolley of the Oversleigh police, an old chum, a reliable man, a diplomat.

'It's my case,' Riley said, grumpy but powerless.

'Agreed. And this is a fact that will not only be impressed upon Mr Jolley, but one that he would quite instinctively respect. You need have no fear, Riley. Jolley, for all his charm and competence, is a man who opted long ago for a quiet life. There is not an ounce of ambition in him. He is that rare thing, a happy man, and happily married to boot. He is a lesson to us all.'

'Very good, sir. But if this Jolley should come up with something . . . '

'Then you shall have your head, Riley, free and untrammelled. I give you my word.'

'Thank you, sir. That's what I wanted to hear.'

'But when and if you are given your head, Riley, it would be so much more effective if you had found a boy, if only to rule him out entirely. Let's you concentrate on the boy, with all your excellent skills and energies, while we await Mr Jolley's conclusions.'

'Yes, sir. I'll get on to it straight away, sir.'

'Excellent. That is what *I* wanted to hear. Now I shall rouse the good Jolley from his contentment and furnish him with the name and address,' he said slowly, deliberately teasing Riley, 'of Miss Ashburton's friend here.' He pointed at the picture, now torn from Karen's pad. 'Thank you, Riley. This is perhaps best done in private. You will, of course, be kept informed.'

He reached for the telephone, knowing that Riley would obey and that he would have given his eye-teeth to know that name and address, so carefully wheedled from the reluctant Miss Ashburton. He smiled with quiet pleasure, as the door closed.

FIVE

Phyllis Luman was not a devout woman, nor would she describe herself as particularly religious, but she was a believer and had experienced the comfort of her faith in the dark first winter of her widowhood. This same belief sustained her during the long period of adjustment to what her son had become. Now she attended the village church irregularly and primarily as a form of social outing. She had not lost her faith, but it had become dormant.

She could not talk to Meg or Paula. Meg would know that Phyllis must do her duty and would be blindly optimistic at the outcome, unable or unwilling to prepare her friend for the worst. Paula would seize the nag of suspicion and elevate it into raging, destructive fact. There was no one else to turn to, except God.

Phyllis knelt in the small church and listened to the birds sing. The church clock above her had just struck seven. The first lilies had bloomed last week and had been used as the centrepiece of Sunday's flowers. Their scent, a little too cloying for Phyllis's taste, hung heavy in the silent, empty church. She tried to pray and could only recite old, ingrained formal prayers. She knotted her hands on the highly polished ledge before her and hoped that their archaic and convoluted language still contained some magic. She remembered the words of a hymn and said them over in her head. God was, as God is wont to be, silent.

'Please,' Phyllis whispered. The birds sang louder and, from the open door to her right, she heard a car pass, changing gear with a rusty sound as it went up the hill. Then she said, 'If it is all in my head . . . Oh, please, God, let it all be in my head. Please.' She rested her head on her hands. Kneeling aggravated the rheumatism in her left knee and she concentrated on the pain, enduring it. Her mind remained blank for a while, the only thing that exercised it – her fear and suspicion – held at bay. For this respite, later, she thanked God and eased herself onto the pew, staring at the altar as she massaged her knee, the leg stuck stiffly out before her. She felt calmer, at least, though she still did not know what to do.

She lingered in the church porch, reading the notices, noting that Mrs Ashburton had been responsible for the lilies, that Meg's group was due to clean the brasses and that Christian Aid week had amassed a total of forty-seven pounds, sixty-three pence in donations.

It was an overcast, muggy morning that threatened later to be blisteringly hot. Phyllis stood and surveyed the sky, looked at the flowers in the neat borders, those on the few remembered graves. She did not, however, walk down the side stone path to the gate but, on impulse, turned right to the arched door that sat in an old stone wall and opened onto the rectory lawn.

Phyllis, like most villagers, had a high regard for the Junes. Faced with the impossibly large and expensive rectory, they had turned it into an open house, a sort of second village hall. Meetings were held in one of the large unused rooms; another held the clutter of the playgroup. They were sociable and lively, the Junes, and they did not force religion down people's throats. Of the two, Phyllis knew Pansy best, for she was a great chatterer and was regularly encountered in the village shop or rushing off on some local errand. Pansy June – it was Paula Brownlow who had announced, soon after Paul took up the living, that she sounded like a cheap film star and looked like an expensive one – was neither a typical nor a comfortable rector's wife. She was nervous, highly strung, instinctively honest and an inveterate gossip. She was also very beautiful, with that uncanny knack given to few women, of being able to make an Oxfam tweed skirt and a hand-knitted twin-set look like a couture outfit. Pansy had alarmed and outraged some people at first, her nervousness often making her strident and clumsy. She had a disconcerting habit of going off into peals of loud giggles even at the bedside of the sick. Not everyone found this cheering. But her openness, generosity and genuine warmheartedness had soon won people over and now Pansy was regarded, yes, as a bit of an eccentric, but a very lovable one.

Paul, in contrast, was staid and stable, a man who thought before he spoke, moved quietly but thoroughly about his pastoral duties. Publically he was perceived as the calm, steady background against which his wife flitted and fluttered, but on his own he was known to be a man of decision, firmness and compassion. Even so, Phyllis hesitated halfway across the rectory lawn, almost turned back. She respected Paul and trusted him. She was genuinely, indulgently fond of Pansy but she had never consulted them on a personal matter. Instinct told her that Paul was the very person, the right and only person to whom she could take her present dilemma, but she was still reluctant. She walked on purposefully. The lawn bordered the drive. It was unlikely that anyone would be at the front of the house so early. She could easily walk away down the drive, with no harm done. And with nothing resolved either, she told herself, and saw another sleepless night looming, another dismal day of fear and anxiety.

Pansy had established the back door, which opened straight into the cavernous kitchen, as the common means of entrance to the house, whether one was making a social visit, delivering jam for the local produce stall or attending Bible Study class. The kitchen, Pansy declared, was the heart of the house, the only warm room in winter and the one that got the most sun in summer. The whole of the back wall of the house was festooned by an old and rampant rambling rose. The door, standing wide open, seemed embowered to Phyllis by heavy yellow blooms as, determined, she moved towards it. The smell of frying bacon and tomatoes, of freshly made coffee drifted out through the doorway, cancelling the perfume of the roses. Nervously, Phyllis tapped and peered in.

Pansy, wielding a frying pan, stood at the great Aga cooker, face flushed, hair sleek, dress pink and summery. The rest of the family were disposed, in various pockets of isolation, around the long refectory table. The pale girl with a startling ring through her nose was the Junes' eldest child, Holly. The unkempt-looking youth with holes in his sweater and very bad acne was the older son, Philip. He and Holly stared, expressionless, at Phyllis. The twins, Andrew and Michael, addressed themselves to plates of puffed wheat with a silent, autonomous diligence. At the head of the table, Paul beamed and, folding his copy of *The Times*, rose politely.

'Phyllis, my dear. How lovely! Look, everybody, here's Mrs Luman come to see us. Come in, come in. What a lovely start to the day,' Pansy said, with genuine pleasure. 'Do sit down. Will you have some breakfast? Oh dear, I haven't enough tomatoes. The price of them! Did you notice? Exorbitant. I could only afford half a pound. I know we ought to grow our own but we never seem to get around to it. But never mind. They'll stretch. Everybody will have just a half . . . '

'No, thank you,' Phyllis said quickly. 'I've already eaten.' This was a lie but Phyllis's stomach contracted at the mere thought of food.

'Oh what a pity. Well, some coffee then. Philip, darling, pour Mrs Luman a cup of coffee. Or would you prefer tea? I can easily . . . ' Bacon and tomatoes were transferred to plates, a kettle lifted and shaken. The scruffy boy rose, scraping his chair on the brick floor, displaying an even larger rent in the seat of his jeans through which scarlet underpants glowed.

'I really don't want to interrupt,' Phyllis apologised, feeling flustered. 'I just called in . . . '

'It's about the fête, isn't it?' Pansy said at once. She pronounced the word in the French manner, not out of ostentation but simply because it was a French word. 'I know I must appear terribly disorganised but honestly I have made masses of lists and everything is sort of under control. Please, do sit down. Milk? Sugar?'

Phyllis sat between one twin and Holly. Philip placed a cup and saucer before her and sank into his chair listlessly. When she sat, Paul sat, still smiling.

'Just milk, thank you.'

'Do you prefer hot? It won't take a moment. Now, where's my milk saucepan?'

Plates were slid in front of Holly and Philip. The latter hacked at a loaf of bread. Both ate with apparent total absorption. Phyllis managed to stop the heating of milk, sipped her coffee, not really listening to Pansy's chatter, until, quietly, Paul said:

'Is there anything I can do for you, Phyllis?'

'Well, yes, actually . . . I wonder if you could spare me a few moments some time? There's something I'd like . . . '

'Oh, but there's no time like the present, is there, darling? You've got fifteen minutes before you have to leave. Will that be long enough, Phyllis? Only Paul's got to go and see the Archdeacon this morning. He's up for the Rural Dean. Oops! I shouldn't have said that. It's desperately secret. But you won't say a word, will you, dear? Isn't it exciting? Anyway, off you both go. Take your coffee with you and be sure to come back and we'll have a proper chat when you've finished.'

Phyllis looked helplessly at Paul who nodded, smiled and said:

'Yes. Let's do that.'

He stood up, carried his cup and newspaper, held the green baize door open for Phyllis.

'I'm so sorry . . . ' she said as he squeezed past her in a narrow, dark corridor.

'Please don't be. This is perfectly convenient. Unless, of course, you'd rather . . . ?'

'No. No, now is fine. If you're sure I'm not . . . '

He held another door open for her, wood and stained glass, which gave onto the square, tiled hall which even in summer felt inhospitably chilly.

'My beloved wife,' he said, heels clicking on the tiles as he overtook Phyllis, 'can be a little overwhelming, but she never really bullies me and she does mean well.'

'I know.'

'Come along, then. At least here we can be quiet.'

His study, at the front of the house, was large and gloomy, the windows overshadowed by trees. The carpet was threadbare, the furniture cheap and ugly. Stuffing was spilling from the easy chair into which he waved Phyllis before perching himself on the edge of the desk and regarding her with a steady, inviting smile.

'That's lovely, about being Rural Dean. Congratulations.'

'Ah, it's not in the bag yet. But if Pansy's wishing it can make it so, then I've already got it.'

'I'm sure. But won't it mean a lot of extra work?'

'Indeed, indeed. But I shall welcome it and, if all else fails, I can always borrow some of Pansy's energy.' She laughed politely at this and he nodded, sighed, seemed for a moment lost in thought about his wife. 'But you know, we both know, you didn't come here to talk about the Rural Dean, whoever he may be.'

'No. I've been to church,' Phyllis did not know why she said this except that perhaps it was a little like offering one's credentials or to forestall him from referring her to God in this matter.

'That's nice. But . . . ?'

'I need advice.'

'Ho-ho. Big word, advice. I've never been good at taking it and I fear I'm worse at giving it. But I can listen and I will tell you what I think. Would you settle for that?' With a touch of Pansy's energy he slid off the desk, swept around it and sat in his creaking, elderly swivel chair.

'It's about Robert,' Phyllis said, putting her cup and saucer down. 'I hardly know how to say it, I feel so disloyal.'

'I am sure you are not being disloyal. Few women, I think, can be as devoted to their sons as you.'

'Thank you. But I . . . well, I . . . I'm sorry. I know you haven't got much time. I'll try to come to the point. I don't know if you've heard about the girl who is missing in Passington?'

'Indeed, yes. Terrible. Terrible.'

'Well, I . . . The thing is, they've issued a description of a man seen near the school. I didn't think anything of it, of course, I hardly listened to it. It was just a verbal description but Paula Brownlow was with me at the time and she noticed . . . You see, the man, the one the police want to trace, he was wearing a blue knitted hat . . . ' She waited, tense, for him to

77

make the same connection, willing him not to. He looked at the top of his desk, as though weighing all she had said.

'Robert is, I am absolutely certain, not the only person to favour blue woolly hats, Phyllis. This must have occurred to you?'

'Of course. As I said, I didn't think anything of it at the time. Paula's quick to jump to conclusions and, well, she isn't very good with Robert. But, you see, there are other things. The jacket, for example, that the man was wearing. It had a lot of zips. Robert has one just like it. That, too, could be a coincidence, of course. It came from a chain store, after all. There must be hundreds of them . . . '

'Quite. Quite.'

'But Robert went out that day, the day the girl disappeared. I let him have days out now and again, by himself. It's good for him to cope on his own. He gets into a bit of a muddle sometimes but . . . Oh, I'm so sorry . . . ' Phyllis surprised herself by beginning to weep.

'My dear, please don't apologise. I can see you're very distressed.'

'I'm all right, really,' Phyllis said, wiping her face with a handkerchief. 'I think it must be the relief of saying it all . . . '

'You've told no one?' She shook her head. 'Then of course it is. And I'm so glad you told me . . . '

'But I haven't finished. You see, even then I knew it couldn't possibly be Robert because he never goes to Passington. He hasn't been there since we came here. The doctors said too many associations might be bad for him, unsettle him. You see, we used to live there, before the accident. He went to school there. I've deliberately kept clear of the place myself. And then, as you know, it's been difficult to get there unless you take the train from Oversleigh and I . . . I don't let him go on trains unaccompanied. He's not used to them. He's fine with buses and then the drivers all know him, they're so very kind . . . '

'Of course. Of course.'

'Only you see now there is a bus service. On Wednesdays. Taylor's coaches.'

'I remember it came up at the PC a while back. It seems there was some demand in the village, but Mrs Blount remarked on the length of the journey and the comparatively short time one has in town. It seems it goes up hill and down dale . . . But as you say, since Robert doesn't go to Passington . . . '

'I found this, in his jacket pocket.' Phyllis opened her purse and took out the pink ticket and slid it across the desk. He stared at it, then, as though making up his mind, picked it up, held it close to his narrowed eyes.

'The twenty-fifth. That was the day . . . '

'Yes.'

'I see.' He lowered the ticket, held it flat between his index fingers on the desk, as though stretching it. 'You must have been sorely tempted to destroy this, Phyllis. Sorely tempted.'

'I wish I could have.'

'Mmm. Understandable.' He continued to stare at the ticket, his head lowered. Phyllis saw that his hair was thinning at the crown, in an appropriate tonsure. She felt better already. She put her handkerchief away but hung on to her purse. 'Now, let us see what we have here,' he said after a while, pushing the ticket back towards her. She picked it up at once. Out of her keeping it seemed even more accusing, damaging. 'All this amounts to, as I see it, is a possibility, a distinct possibility, admittedly, that Robert went to Passington on the day the girl disappeared, on the day a man somewhat vaguely resembling Robert, was seen near the school. Did he return by the Passington bus? You could tell from the time, presumably?'

'No. Much later. Ken Cartwright gave him a lift from Oversleigh.'

'And how does Robert explain this?'

'Well, he doesn't. His memory isn't quite . . . '

'Have you questioned him closely, Phyllis?'

'Yes. He says, sometimes he went to Anderton, as he intended to do, and missed the bus back. He's done that before, that's not unlikely. As I said, sometimes he gets muddled. So he got the bus to Oversleigh and started to walk. He's done that before, too . . . '

'You said, "sometimes" . . . '

'When I've said, "Did you go to Passington?" sometimes, if he answers at all, he says, "Yes. Passington."'

'Well, then . . . We know that he could have done so and the ticket would certainly seem to point to that. But how did he get to Oversleigh? There's no bus service as I recall.'

'He could have caught the train. He *could* have. It's possible.'

'But that would have been a considerable adventure for Robert. Surely he would have told you about it?'

'Of course. But . . . if he has something to hide . . . '

'Oh dear, oh dear. What a terrible thing this uncertainty is. Phyllis, I do understand. I'm so glad you came to me. And you realise that I must ask you . . . '

'Robert wouldn't hurt a fly,' she said quickly, to get it over with, to save embarrassment. 'He couldn't. Oh, I know he has rages – much less so now than he used, hardly at all, in fact . . . But even when he was very bad in that way, he never harmed or struck a person. It was only frustration. If he couldn't understand something or make something work, he might damage it, smash it . . . The doctors said it was just frustration, because he had been such a competent boy, you see, and maybe there's some memory left, some vague knowledge that he could make things work, once . . . '

'I understand. Please, please, don't distress yourself.'

'So I know, whatever, wherever he went, he wouldn't hurt anyone, least of all a girl . . . '

'But there is no suggestion, is there, that the poor girl has been harmed?'

'They said last night, on the wireless, that they feared for her safety. They did another big search yesterday, all around Passington but they found nothing. Naturally, they must think . . . '

'Oh dear. How very sad. And no wonder you had a sleepless night. It shows on your face, my dear . . . '

'I'm sorry . . . '

'Please, please . . . '

'Anyway, you see, the very last person he'd harm, if he ever should harm anyone, would be a girl, especially a stranger. He's afraid of girls, really. Perhaps that's not the right word. In awe of them. He really doesn't know anything about them. The only girl he ever knew at all well was Mrs Ashburton's daughter. She was so good and patient with him. He doesn't have the normal feelings, you see, that men have for girls. In that respect he's still and always will be a child.'

'Not the sort of person, then, who would easily get into conversation with a stranger, go off with them?'

'Absolutely not. He's very shy. And his speech . . . '

'Quite, quite. Then why are we perplexing ourselves? Because suspicion is a terrible thing. It gnaws. And you are afraid, aren't you, Phyllis, that if you do nothing, someone, someone less . . . sensible than Mrs Brownlow might jump to a similar conclusion?'

'Exactly,' she said, with real relief.

'Then there is only one thing to be done as I see it.'

'Go to the police, you mean?'

'I fear so. "Fear" only because it will probably mean some . . . disruption for Robert. They will probably want to talk to him, to verify the facts, so to speak. But then I think he could cope with that, with you by his side, don't you?'

'I . . . expect so. You think I should . . . ?'

He held up his hand, partly so that he could check the time by his watch, partly to silence her.

'Do you know our Constable Smith well?'

'Hardly at all. I've seen him around, of course . . . '

'Well, even though he's only been here, what, a matter of six months or so, he's impressed Pansy and me very favourably. And Mrs Blount, too. She said to me, only the other day, that he's got the village-bobby mentality. He's quiet and steady and tactful. Now, what I suggest is, that you leave this to me. I shall be back from seeing the Archdeacon by six at the very latest. If you wish, I'd be very happy to give Arthur Smith a call and then perhaps you and I could pop along and see him later this evening. What do you say?'

'You'd come with me?'

'If you would welcome my presence, I should be delighted.'
He came around the desk, holding his arm out, inviting her to rise, ready to usher her to the door.

'I would be so grateful. It would make me feel so much better.'

'Then it's as good as done. I shall telephone you as soon after six as possible.'

'I don't know how to thank you.'

'My dear Phyllis . . . '

'Thank you so much.'

'God bless you.' He opened the door, then half-closed it. Conspiratorially, he said, 'I doubt you feel up to one of Pansy's chats just now. Slip out the front door and I'll make your excuses.'

'Thank you.' Tears of gratitude and relief filled her eyes and made her feel foolish. Already she felt there was no substance to her fears. Paul June had already drained them of their corrosive acid and later, soon, PC Smith would cancel them entirely.

'Until this evening, then,' he called, one hand raised in a salute or blessing as she walked with a lighter tread down the drive and away from the rectory.

Jolley sat in his unmarked car, smiling, thinking that the village was very attractive. He and Eileen had considered it a while back, when they had decided to treat his retirement as more imminent than it was. With property prices rising the way they were, it made sense to buy now even if it did stretch them financially for a bit. Jolley would have settled for the village – they had had an excellent grilled trout in the only pub, he remembered – but Eileen had set her heart on Clifton Kings. She had always liked it and it was much more convenient for Passington, the shops, little runs out to local beauty spots. Jolley was content.

He looked at the bungalow and thought that he really did not understand why his daughter poured such venomous scorn on 'bungaloids' as she called them. The charms of her converted barn were somewhat lost on him, for that is exactly what it felt like – a barn. But as Eileen was fond of saying, 'It's a good job we're not all alike. That would make for a very dull world.' He could easily imagine a time when he and Eileen would be glad not to have to climb stairs. Bungalows were all right and this one, he thought, was a right little cracker. Modern but not odd. Obviously convenient and very well kept. He liked the symmetrical rows of roses flanking the concrete path. He liked the front door being set bang slap in the middle and the crinkly grey slates, the way they caught the soft evening sunlight. But he was not paid to sit and gawp, he reminded himself, and eased his bulk out of the suddenly unpleasantly hot car. He had a delicate, diplomatic mission to perform and he should have been preparing himself for that, not idling, relishing the finer things of life.

He liked, too, the way the big window was not made all private by lace curtains. It spoke of an open person, with nothing to hide. His eye, though, noted that the corresponding window, that on the left of the door, was curtained. A bedroom, he supposed, and therefore understandable. He must have been staring at that window for, as he unlatched the gate, the curtain was tweaked aside and a face appeared. There was nothing furtive about the movement. This was not the action of someone trying to avoid the tally-man or the rent collector. And the face that stared at him was not that of some nosy old parker. He recognised it at once and doing so gave a sharper edge to his mission. Jolley's smiling eyes became narrower, more alert. Karen Ashburton, whom he knew slightly, a photocopy of whose drawing of the face he carried in his document case, had done an excellent job. The fact that she had, only made the whole situation more complicated. Then, as he closed the gate and started up the path, the watching face changed, seemed to melt and become watery. The curtain dropped back into place. Fear? he asked himself, but did not think so. A simple loss of interest, he would say. Perhaps a failure of concentration. But then he was distracted by the shadowy appearance of a form behind the rippled glass of the front door. Again there was something watery about it, as though some motif were being stressed or repeated. Before Jolley could find the bell-push, the door opened and Phyllis Luman stared anxiously at him.

He would always think of her, could only describe her as a tidy little body, sharp and bright. Despite the warmth of the evening, she wore a light coat over her floral dress, neat court shoes that set off a still trim ankle. Her hair was brushed and there was a light coating of make-up on her face. Jolley introduced himself, smiling.

'This is an unofficial visit,' he stressed.

'But I'm expecting to go out at any minute,' she protested, flustered and preoccupied. 'I'm just waiting for the rector to phone now.' She looked over her shoulder at the telephone.

'I'm sure this won't take long. It's about your son. Robert, isn't it?'

At this her head snapped towards him and he needed no training, no experience to see that he had touched on a raw nerve.

'I don't understand . . . '

'If I might just come in I'd be happy to explain . . . '

'The police, you say?'

'Oversleigh police, yes. But, as I said, this is an unofficial visit . . . '

'But we were just going to see Constable Smith. The rector's going to ring . . . '

He knew Smith and said so, asked again to be let in.

'I don't understand how you knew – know,' she said, stepping back to admit him. He closed the door behind him, followed her into the sitting room. Comfortable, neat, a thoroughly pleasant room, he thought. She stood before the empty grate, twisting her hands together. He noticed cotton gloves and a handbag that matched her shoes standing ready on the arm of a chair. 'We were just going to see Constable Smith,' she repeated.

'Perhaps you'd better tell me about that first,' he suggested. 'I might be able to save you a trip.'

She hesitated. She thought, Oh, what does it matter? This man knew something, had come looking for Robert. She had always believed that it was best to make a clean breast of things and so she told him, told him substantially, but in a more ordered fashion, what she had told Paul June that morning. Again it was a relief to say it and something about Jolley's watchful, smiling countenance kept promising that he would burst out laughing and so blow all her doubts away. Then the telephone rang.

'That'll be the rector now. Excuse me.'

'Perhaps he might like a word with me,' Jolley suggested, moving to let her pass. He thought he understood the situation. What she had told him put a different complexion on it all, of course, but he saw no cause for alarm, was glad that vicars still had time and the interest to extend pastoral care beyond the routinely religious.

She pushed the door open and said, 'Mr . . . er . . . ?'

'Jolley.'

'The rector would like a word.'

Phyllis had tried to listen to what he said but her mind was frightened by big, threatening words like 'Passington' and 'Superintendent'. She thought that she was going to scream and told herself not to be so silly. Then she was holding the receiver again and heard Paul June say, ' . . . a sound man. I know him slightly. I'm sure you did right to tell him. Would you like me to come over?'

'We're not going to see Mr Smith?'

'No. There's no need now. Mr Jolley will explain everything to you. Now, shall I come over?'

'Oh no. No, please don't trouble yourself.'

'Well, promise you'll ring me when you've finished with Mr Jolley. And if you want either of us, Pansy's here as well . . . '

'Yes. Yes, thank you. I'd better go now.' She only understood that she did not have to go out now. But she had told this man, this Jolley, all she knew. She went back into the room and met his smile with an anxious, confused look. 'I'm sorry, I just don't understand.'

'Why don't we sit down?' he said, moving towards Paula's chair. 'And then I'll explain.'

When she sat down, she became aware of the coat, pulled it around her, looked embarrassed. She managed a small smile when Jolley stood up and helped her off with it, placed it on the sofa.

'Thank you,' she said, 'I thought I was going out, you see. I . . . '

'It's all right, Mrs Luman. Now let me explain.' As he did so, it sounded odd and unconvincing to his ears, but Phyllis Luman seemed to accept it without question. He kept Karen Ashburton's name out of it, as the Superintendent had instructed, to avoid village gossip, animosity. 'So, you see, it is the difference of opinion between the witness and the artist that made the Superintendent feel that we should . . . er . . . have this little chat first.'

'I see,' she said. Then, sharply, 'What do you mean, "first"? Before what?'

'Well, Mrs Luman, I'm afraid that what you've told me does mean that Passington will want to talk to your son . . . ' She covered her face with her hands, stifling a little cry of distress. 'Please don't upset yourself, Mrs Luman. I'm sure there's no need. Unless, of course, there is something you haven't told me?'

'No. Nothing at all. It's not that. It's Robert. They won't know how to . . . He's not normal, Mr Jolley. He can't answer questions, not your sort of questions. It will upset him terribly.'

'I'm sure,' he said, crossing his fingers, 'they'll be very gentle and patient. You see,' he said, leaning forward and smiling, 'what you must remember is that they just want to rule Robert out. This witness saw Robert – or someone very like him . . . Just a minute.' He unzipped his document case and pulled out the photostat of Karen Ashburton's picture and handed it to her. She gasped with recognition and surprise. 'Now, if Robert can just confirm that he was near the school that morning, or not as the case may be . . . He might have seen the missing girl, you see. He might be able to help us. You'd want him to do that if he can, wouldn't you?'

She gave the drawing back to him.

'But what if he can't? What if he can't remember? What then?' she asked urgently.

He was going to say, Let's cross that bridge when we come to it, but knew that was inadequate, would in no way reassure her. He groped for the right words.

'I'll have a word with the Superintendent. I'm sure if they fully understand the position . . . It would help if I could see Robert. Could I meet him? I should very much like to.'

'Yes, yes,' she said, obviously grasping at straws. 'I'm sure that would be best.'

Instinctively, Jolley followed her, did not wait politely for her to bring Robert in. She did not appear to think this odd, but at his door, on the opposite side of the hall, she hesitated, turned nervously towards Jolley and said, 'You will be gentle with him? He hasn't done anything wrong. I know he hasn't.'

'As gentle as a lamb,' Jolley said, smiling. She nodded, tapped on the door, opened it.

'Robert? Here's someone wants to meet you. Mr Jolley.'

He could barely squeeze into the room, so cluttered and crowded was it. Robert was sitting on the bed, the only place to sit, as far as Jolley could tell, surrounded by American comics, a large, untidy pile of which also occupied the bedside table. He wore a singlet, dark trousers and the blue hat. He looked at Jolley without curiosity or interest, made some guttural, throaty noise that might have been, 'Hello.'

'Hello, Robert. How are you?' Jolley suppressed the natural instinct to offer his hand, realised that he still carried the photocopy.

'All right.' He turned back to his comics.

'Mr Jolley wants to ask you some questions, dear,' Phyllis said, moving around the amplifier to stand close to him. With him, Jolley noted, she became calm, almost what he imagined would be her normal self. 'Put those away for a minute.' She bent and started tidying the comics.

'No,' he said, and patted at her hand.

'Please, Robert . . . ' She sounded tired.

'Nice room you've got here, Robert. Lots of nice things.'

Robert stared at the comic, opened across his knees.

'Nice,' he said.

'I don't expect you want to get out much, having so many nice things to . . . ' Just in time, Jolley stopped himself saying 'to play with'. Phyllis's eyes hardened, were fixed on him. ' . . . to keep you busy,' he finished lamely. He cleared his throat. 'Still, I was wondering if you've been into town recently . . . '

'Thursday,' he said quickly, grumpily, still staring at the comic.

'We always go into Oversleigh on Thursdays,' Phyllis explained. 'There's a bus . . . ' Jolley nodded.

'I was thinking more of Anderton,' he said to the bent, blue head. 'Or Passington.'

'Me?' Robert asked.

'Yes, dear. You remember . . . '

'No.'

'Oh. Somebody must be mistaken then,' Jolley said. 'Somebody thought they saw you there recently. Somebody thought they recognised you.'

It seemed to Jolley that Robert started to shake his head, although an involuntary twitch could not be ruled out. Then slowly his head came round, his eyes focused on Jolley, uncertain but with a light dawning in them.

'Recognise? Me?'

'Yes, that's right. Is that possible?'

'Somebody recognise me,' he said, pleased, looking towards his mother. Barely she managed to smile and nod encouragement.

'Yes, dear,' she said.

'Recognise . . . ' He sounded like he was tasting the word, trying to identify it. Jolley felt that he was slipping away, saw his eyes slide back, almost covertly, to the comic.

'Yes, indeed. So much so that they were able to draw a picture of you. Here.' Jolley thrust the picture at him. It had the desired effect, caught his attention.

'Picture of me?' he asked uncertainly.

'That's right. Take a look. Is that you?'

Very slowly, as though it might burn or bite him, Robert swivelled his eyes to the picture. Then, with a burst of energy that made Jolley jump, he snatched it, held it close to his eyes for a moment or two, then lowered it. It was painful to watch the pleasure on his face, the sheer, childish delight.

'Me,' he breathed. 'Picture me . . .' Then he darted from the bed, knocking into Phyllis who had to put a hand out to steady herself and peered at his reflection in the mirror. She looked, pained, at Jolley, who could only smile. Robert held the picture up in front of him, studied it, lowered it, saw himself, repeated the process, blocking his image out with a square of white paper. 'Picture, Mam. Look, Mam. Picture. Me. Yes, yes, yes.'

'Yes, dear, yes,' she said.

'It's very good. Very like you,' Jolley said and wondered if this was tantamount to a leading question.

'Good,' Robert agreed. 'Very good,' nodding and smiling at the drawing held stretched between his hands.

'Yes, dear. Now give it back to Mr Jolley.'

'No,' he shouted, the single syllable ringing in their ears. He crushed the picture to his chest, clamped it there with both arms. Advancing his face close to his mother's, he shouted, 'Me. Mine. Mine. Mine.'

'No, dear, it's Mr Jolley's. You must . . .'

'I think we can let him keep it,' Jolley said quickly, moved and rather frightened.

'Oh, but . . .'

'I really don't see why not.'

'Mine,' Robert murmured, head bent low to the clutched drawing.

Jolley nodded at Phyllis, indicating that it was all right, really.

'Nice meeting you, Robert,' he said. 'I'll see you again very soon.' He had an eerie feeling that he did not exist. Robert frowned as his mother moved, obviously fearing that she would try to take the picture from him. She touched his hunched, protective shoulder.

'It's all right, dear. Mr Jolley says you can keep the picture.'

'Picture. Me. Mine,' he repeated through a bubble of saliva.

Jolley shook his head sadly and hoped that Phyllis Luman did not see.

That nice Mr Jolley, as Phyllis already thought of him, fetched and accompanied them to Passington. Overnight Phyllis Luman appeared to have got a hold on herself. Jolley could not know, of course, about Paul June's wise counsel, the long talk she had had with Meg Sowers, but he was right to suspect that the fundamental change had come from herself, her own strength. Phyllis Luman had faced much worse before and shown herself to be strong and resourceful. She was good at accepting facts, easily panicked by fantasy and speculation. Paul June had pointed out that her fears were foundless, that there was no body, no whisper of evidence that harm had befallen the missing girl. There was only the possibility that Robert had been noticed and remembered at the place where the girl was last seen. It was a sad, sad reflection on the times, Meg had said, that we have come to expect the worst, do not even look for the best. It would be an ordeal for Robert, yes, but it would all be over in a few hours. Phyllis clung to that. And no harm done. Accordingly, she had dressed in her powder-blue suit and wore a rather jaunty little hat, on which Jolley was quick to compliment her.

To Robert the whole trip seemed like one big adventure, an unexpected journey in a fast, smooth car, Mam all dressed up and smiling. What he thought about Jolley, whether he connected the fat, smiling man with the gift of the picture that so delighted him, was unknowable, but he took for some reason an enthusiastic shine to the uniformed driver to whom he tried, in his own way, to chat. The young man responded cheerfully, apparently content not to understand.

Jolley began to feel better. He had known, long before he rang Superintendent Teddy Tait, that the boy – Jolley had no hesitation in so designating Robert Luman – would have to be questioned. He had hoped to do it at Oversleigh, to do it himself, but there was protocol as well as procedure to be observed, Detective Inspector Riley's *amour-propre* to be considered. Jolley had no choice but to accept, to be the gracious recipient of Tait's effusive thanks, but he remained determined to make it as painless as possible for the Lumans, the best of a bad job, he called it, though Eileen had told him not to be so cynical. If the boy knew anything, he doubted they would ever get it out of him, at least not in any coherent way. He had warned Tait of this and had asked him to apprise Riley of it. As for the possibility that Robert Luman might be seriously involved in the case, Jolley did not even consider this. Even if the girl turned up as a body and Robert made a full confession which was confirmed by witnesses, any solicitor worth his fee would have no difficulty in pleading incompetence. Incompetent, Jolley thought, and incapable, too. There he sat, grinning like a great, daft kid, bouncing on the back seat, chattering in his own inimitable way. Jolley transferred his smile to Phyllis Luman, wished that he could pat her hand reassuringly.

Robert continued to enjoy himself when they reached Passington police station. He liked the way people kept looking at him, all the handshaking that went on, from which he did not at all mind being excluded. People here did not stare at him as though there was something wrong, but stole glances, covertly. It fitted in his mind with something the fat man who smiled a lot had said. The word 'recognised' danced in his mind and pleased him. Consequently, Robert tried to be very careful, to say 'please' and 'thank you', to pay attention and behave. Mam said there were people who wanted to talk to him. Robert liked talking to people. He was to tell them anything they wanted to know. This worried Robert a bit because he did not know what that was, but it was a fleeting worry. His mind's eye conjured up images of rows of microphone things and bright lights and he went very happily into the interview room, flanked by a uniformed constable and another man who opened the door for him, pausing only to wave and smile at Mam.

Riley felt it the moment he entered the interview room and looked at Robert. At first he thought the totally unexpected shock he felt was due to Karen Ashburton's skill, that it was the simple shock of recognition, like when you see royalty or a film star in the flesh for the first time and discover that they really do look like their photographs, animated and made three-dimensional. Oh there was no doubt that Karen had 'got' him all right, but it was what she had left out that shook Riley and made him break out in an unpleasant sweat. She had left out that he was 'wrong'. The features were there, the planes and shadows, the ridiculous woolly hat which turned out to be blue, just as Tracy had maintained, but Karen had shown them fixed and pertinent, 'normal'. What he saw was a face that threatened disintegration at any moment. A face wearing a smile that seemed to have a life of its own, which, Riley thought, could slide off his face and onto his shoulder, skitter about his chest and onto the desk like some ghastly slug-like creature. Riley squeezed his eyes shut, heard Sergeant Williams clear his throat loudly, Constable Jennings shift his feet. He opened his eyes and wiped his palms on his thighs. The face was now blank and vapid, the eyes misted, elsewhere.

'Er . . . you . . . Are you Robert Godfrey Luman?' he said, his voice sounding like he'd gargled with gravel. It seemed to take forever before the words got through – got through to what? Riley's mind screamed – and the grin came back, steadied.

'Robert,' it said and nodded its head too hard, in a wobbly sort of way that need not and probably never would stop.

'Right,' Riley said loudly. 'You, Jennings, get his . . . get his particulars. I'll . . . er . . . be back in a minute.'

It had always been there but he had never had to face it, not really. Standing in the washroom, trying to get a grip on himself, Riley did not know what it was. It was like one of those irrational phobias, he supposed, that strong grown men still fall prey to – a fluttering moth, a scuttling spider, the swooping glide of a bat. He had never been able to handle disability, was one of those who stuffed too much money into rattling collecting tins, his face averted, who could not look at certain posters imploring charity. Common sense said it had something

92

to do with Aunt Maura's kid, the awful, mongoloid thing they thrust under his nose when he was a boy of eleven and had told him to hold. But Riley found it equally uncomfortable to believe that a part of his life, his personality, could be shaped by a childhood incident. He thrust that thought away as fiercely as he had pushed at the awful baby. It was just one of those things, he told himself, drying his hands. The only way to deal with it was to forget about it, pretend that it wasn't there, didn't exist.

He emerged from the washroom a man of purpose. There was work to be done. He ignored the baleful stare of Tracy Vorlander, squashed on a bench with her sullen mother and was deaf to the instant complaint of Kevin Walker, a driver with the Taylor Coach Company, who had been cooling his heels and chain-smoking for half an hour in the corridor. He went through the open-plan office like a man who had just sighted his quarry and sat at his desk almost out of breath. There was – there always was – a pile of routine paperwork and he pulled the tray towards him, ignoring the fact that his hands trembled. There was escape, solace, satisfaction in work, dull, routine work. He uncapped his pen and attacked the papers like a junior out to impress his superiors. And he grew calmer as he became absorbed. He did not even bother to look up at the tap on his door.

'Yes?'

'Sorry, sir. It's Luman, sir. I can't seem to . . . I mean, I can't get any sense out of him, sir.'

'You can't—' He looked up at Jennings, his face a mask of anger. The young man blushed. 'Use your nous, Jennings. Just for once, will you?' He stood up and walked around his desk. 'Get the mother in, lad. Get the details from her.' He looked around the larger office, spotted an empty desk in the corner by the window, which framed a less spectacular version of the view from Tait's office above. 'Bring them up here. Use that desk. And get on with it.'

'Yes, sir.'

Kill two birds with one stone, he thought. Decisive action. Get on with it. Get through it. Heads turned as he strode back through the office. WPC Hignett dived to prevent a carbon copy being swept up in the wind of his progress. She rolled her eyes and put her head down.

'Right, sorry to keep you waiting,' Riley said, confronting the obese Vorlanders, the impatient, pacing Walker.

'I have got a job to go to, you know,' Walker said, dropping another cigarette stub onto the floor and grinding it out with his heel.

'Then we'll take you first, Mr Walker,' Riley said. 'In a few minutes, I'm going to ask you to walk quite casually through the office in there.' He pointed to the swing door which still flapped with the speed and force of his exit. 'I want you to pay particular attention to the desk in the far left corner, by the window. Don't make it obvious. Don't say anything. Just take your time, have a good look and go straight into my office at the end. Got that?'

'Yeah.'

'If you need more time, just tell me quietly. Don't make a fuss. The same goes for you, Tracy. Do you understand? Do you know what to do?'

'What?'

He explained it again, slowly, aware of Walker champing restlessly behind him. He felt, for once, almost grateful to Tracy Vorlander. Her slowness was familiar, comforting. When, at last, she appeared to understand, he moved to the door and glanced through the square pane of glass set in it, saw that Jennings and the Lumans were in place.

'Right. Mr Walker, if you please.' He swept the door open, grinned at Tracy who looked startled and followed Walker into the office. The young man walked steadily, not hurrying, not dawdling, his eyes fixed on the corner of the room. When he drew more or less level with the desk at which Jennings sat, head bent, hand writing, Riley caught him up, said, 'OK?' and, receiving a token nod, steered Walker into his office, closing the door behind him. 'Well?'

'That's him all right.'

'You're sure?'

94

'I'm not likely to forget a wally like that, am I?'

'I didn't ask for comments, Walker, just a positive identification.'

Walker sighed heavily.

'That's the chap got on my coach at Brindsleigh that morning. The twenty-fifth. Now can I go?'

'You're prepared to swear that, on oath, in a court of law?'

'If I have to, yes.'

'Thank you.'

'Now can I go?'

'Just tell me again, tell me what you remember.'

'Oh, for God's sake—'

'The sooner we get through this, the sooner you can go, all right?'

'All right. OK. I'm on the Oversleigh to Passington village run that morning. I left the depot in Oversleigh about eight forty-five a.m., got to the Brindsleigh stop just before eight fifty-five. I remember I was a bit early, so I settled down for a wait. There was no one at the stop but some of the old dears that use that service are a bit slow, so if you've got time in hand, you wait. That's instructions. Then this chap comes running up – him. He gets on and I remember thinking he looks a real wally, wearing that blue hat on a hot day. He asked for a return and I said, "One eighty," and he queried it. "One forty," he said. Well, I twigged he was a bit simple or something so I asked him if he was sure he wanted my bus. The regular service to Anderton's due at five past, see, and the fare's one forty. But, no, he says he wants this bus so I gives him a ticket and off we go. Now can—'

'Do you remember seeing him leave the bus?'

'Yes. He got out of his seat before we reached the bus station at Passington. There's always one, breaking their necks to get off. He was doing some pushing and shoving down the front, right by my cab. You see, once one makes a rush for it, they all start. I was going to tell him to pack it in but some old woman tells him so I left 'em to it. Anyway, he was first off. And I've never seen him again until this morning. But that's

95

him, sitting out there, with the blue hat on.'

'Thank you very much, Mr Walker. You may go.'

Riley followed him back through the office but did not even glance at the Lumans. He collected Tracy, told Mrs Vorlander to walk with her, opened the door for them and watched them squeeze through. They lumbered, he thought. Tracy looked around her, looked everywhere but where she was told to. He had a sudden vision of himself on a treadwheel of his own making, pacing up and down the length of this room for eternity, waiting for Tracy Vorlander to get it right.

She let out a single, sharp shriek, turned and buried her head in her mother's vast bosom.

'Now look what you've done,' Mrs Vorlander said as he hurried up to her. His eyes met those of Robert Luman, staring, grinning, finding the whole scene a source of amusement.

'All right. All right. Come along, now.' Riley got them into his office, encouraged Mrs Vorlander to calm Tracy which she did by pushing her roughly away and telling her to shut up and stop showing her up.

Tracy's cry had been sufficient, but he had to get it out of her in more easily transcribable terms.

'Yes. Yes, yes,' she said at last. 'Oh, Mum, I want to go home.'

So did Riley.

He came shuffling into the room. Whatever contorted pleasure he had taken in the process so far had evidently worn off. He looked bored. Probably the high spot of his day was Tracy's scream, Riley thought, deliberately not looking at him. Perhaps he liked making little girls scream.

'Sit down, Mr Luman.' Jennings hovered behind him, pulled out the chair for him and made him sit. Jennings remained hovering. Riley stared at the form in front of him. 'You are Robert Godfrey Luman of The Bungalow, forty-eight Brindsleigh Village?' He waited.

'Just answer "yes", Robert. Say "yes" when Mr Riley asks you.'

'Yes,' said Robert.

'And you are a British citizen, unmarried and are thirty-one years of age?'

Robert said nothing. Riley looked up. Jennings said, 'His mum swears to it all, sir. I think you can take it as read.'

'Thank you, Jennings,' Riley said. Jennings was good with him, took it in his stride. He hated Jennings. 'Now, Mr Luman, I have two persons who are prepared to swear that they saw you on the morning of the twenty-fifth, one on the bus to Passington and the other outside Passington Upper School at about eleven thirty. What do you have to say to that?'

Robert stared at his hands.

'I think that's a bit complicated for him, sir. You have to keep it simple.'

Riley suppressed a desire to overturn the table and sock Jennings on the jaw.

'Very well. Let's try it your way.' He hitched his chair into the table and in a false, sing-song said, 'Well now, Robert. I know two people who say they saw you in Passington the other week. Were you there?' Robert shook his head, no. 'You must have been, Robert, because these two people saw you. They recognised you . . . '

His head came up. A slow, different kind of smile spread over his face, giving a kind of steadiness to his lips.

'Recognise,' he said. 'Recognise me.' And nodded, cheerful and definite.

'Good. Good. So if they recognised you, Robert, you must have been there, mustn't you?'

He went on smiling, then turned to look at Jennings who nodded. Robert burst out laughing and went on laughing.

Riley could only stare at him, fighting his own instinct to run. Jennings bent over Robert, soothing him, muttering something. Robert's laughter died away. He looked at Riley.

'Not . . . not . . . invisible man,' he said and beamed triumphantly.

'I think you could say he understands, sir. Sort of,' Jennings offered.

97

'Would you like to conduct this bloody interview, Jennings? You looking for my job or something?'

'No, sir. Sorry, sir.'

'Then bloody well button it.'

'Yes, sir.'

'Zip,' Robert said and felt with his left hand for the zip on his bomber jacket. His hand encountered rough tweed, an open pocket.

'Did you go by the school, Robert?' Riley asked. 'Passington Upper School?'

'Big School.'

'That's right. You – were – there?'

Robert nodded, tried to remember, but it all got jumbled up, saw himself entering the other school, his hand in his father's hand.

'Listen, Robert. I'm going to tell you a story. You like stories, don't you?'

'Great,' said Robert, wriggling in his chair with excitement.

'Good. This is a story about you, Robert. About the day you got the bus from Brindsleigh into Passington and went – went to the Big School, right?'

'Yes.'

'Good. And while you were there you saw a girl. You like girls, Robert? Do you? Like girls?'

'Yes.'

'You saw a nice girl come out of the school and . . . '

'Field,' said Robert.

'No, girl—'

'Field. Hayfield. Long grass.'

Riley saw it then, the field, opposite the school, the long waving grass which had been ruined now by his men trampling it, combing it for any sign, clue to the whereabouts of Lenora Mitchell. The farmer was threatening to sue for compensation.

'What about the field, Robert?' Robert stared at him blinking rapidly. 'You went into the field, didn't you, Robert? Did the girl go with you, Robert?'

'No. No. Not field.'

'Where then, Robert? Where did you take her?'

'Hayfield. Don't go in hayfield. Bad. Bad girl.'

'You saw the girl in the field, did you? Is that it?'

Robert tried to think, tried very hard to think, but there was nothing there but a bad feeling, a wrong feeling. He said: 'Mam?'

'In a minute, Robert. Let me finish my story first.'

'Story.'

'Yes. The story about you and this girl. Did you know her name, Robert?'

'No girl.'

'Yes, there was a girl, Robert. And you went with her into the field.' Riley opened a folder on which, so far, he had rested his hands. He took out the blown-up photograph of Lenora Mitchell and turned it, slowly, to face Robert. 'This girl.'

Robert stared at it, stared at her. As he stared, not understanding, her features shifted and took on life. He drew back with a start, offended.

'Didn't ought to do that,' he said. 'No.' He saw the girl with her two fingers savagely raised towards him, her pretty face ugly with temper and rudeness. 'Not my fault,' Robert said sadly. There was something else, something nicer, something funny. He could not remember. He looked up at Riley and tried very hard to remember because that was what Riley wanted. He was tired and wanted to go to sleep. It wasn't fun any more. He wanted to go to Mam, to go home. The girl faded back into her colourless photograph where she dimpled and smiled.

'Knickers,' Robert said suddenly, very pleased with himself. He began to laugh.

'What about her knickers, Robert? Come on. You can tell me. Fun was it? Nice?'

'Funny,' he said and laughed very happily.

'Funny?' Riley said, dangerously. He caught himself in time, made his fist unclench. He put the photograph away, buying time. Obviously Luman recognised her, knew her. When he felt that his voice would be steady, Riley spoke into the silence left by Robert's laughter. 'What about her knickers, Robert?' But when he looked at him, he saw that Robert had gone, had removed himself somewhere. He was patting himself urgently, patting his chest, his sides, his thighs in a haphazard manner that made Riley's nerve snap. 'Stop that!' he shouted. 'Keep still!' Robert's left hand closed over his packet of cigarettes, lost in one of the pockets of the unfamiliar best jacket. He was still as though responding to Riley's shout. 'That's better,' Riley said. Then Robert pulled out the packet of Marlboro and fished one out, stuck it in his mouth and started the awful, manic patting again. 'What the hell do you think you're doing?' Riley said, jumping to his feet, his chair scraping on the floor. Jennings took a step forward, froze. 'No smoking in here. No smoking.' Robert found his lighter, pulled it out, flicked it. Nothing happened. He flicked it again. 'I said . . . ' The flame appeared, shot up and Riley lunged forward, making the table rock. He chopped the side of his hand into Robert's, sending the lighter flying. Robert looked at him, totally bemused. Riley's face was inches from his, pale with anger and tension. Robert was afraid.

'Ciggie,' he said and the movement of his lips made the cigarette drop onto the table.

'I said no smoking,' Riley breathed.

Robert tried to retrieve the cigarette but Riley was quicker. He brought his fist down on it, squashing it. The frail white paper burst and shreds of tobacco exploded outwards. Robert stared in amazement.

'Ciggie,' he said, his voice rising, demanding. 'Ciggie.'

'Shut up,' Riley said. 'Just shut up.' He drew back looking at the terrible face, working with some obscene life of its own. Half-child, half-man, poised between tears and anger. Riley felt sick with fear. 'And, for Christ's sake, take that bloody hat off when you're talking to me.' He snatched the hat, yanked it from Robert's head and threw it across the room.

Robert exploded into action then. He stood up, and as he did so, hurled the table from him so that it fell over, making Riley dance backward, the crashing table narrowly missing his toes. Robert stumbled forward, hit the table, stopped. Then he made a terrible sound, a child's scream of incomprehension, an

100

animal's wail of agony. He threw his arms upward and clasped them across his head, holding and hugging it. Riley saw nothing but his ugly, fat tears, the sickly dribble running from his mouth, over his chin, onto his jacket.

All things considered, Riley had got off pretty lightly. The old man could have chewed him up and spat out the bones. For some reason he had been content merely to wound, lacerate and threaten.

'I don't understand you. You've always been a . . . competent officer, Riley, therefore you must know that nothing poor Mr Luman might manage – with a lot of help, no doubt – to tell you would ever stand up in court. Any solicitor would be able to elicit a contradictory statement, at the very least.'

'I know,' Riley said, thumping his right fist into his left palm for emphasis, 'that Luman knows something. You can't deny he recognised Lenora Mitchell's photograph. Jennings was there. He saw. I know Luman had something to do with it . . . '

'There you go again, "with it", with what? What is this "it" you and you alone, apparently, know so much about? Won't you share it with me at least?'

'You know she's dead as well as I do,' Riley said, disgusted. He didn't care any more. He pushed his hands in his trouser pockets and went to the window, stood there, ignoring the Superintendent, looking out. Tait let the silence stretch. He did not use the time to weigh the pros and cons or examine his own course of action. He simply waited until Riley became calmer or bored with the view. At first sign of this – a sigh, a slight shifting of his stance – Tait began to speak, in a low, flat, rapid monotone.

'What we have here is a case of a missing person. You and anyone working with you forget that at your peril. You are not paid to speculate or – what is that awful phrase? – "play hunches". Indeed, in my force, you will do neither. Nor will you intimidate witnesses or assault them . . . '

'I snatched his bloody hat off, that's all . . . ' Riley burst out, swinging round to face him.

'Am I to understand from that that you were trying to teach him some manners?'

'Something like that.' He turned away again, sullenly, Tait thought.

'Then that is how it will appear in the report but only because it will never, ever happen again.' He waited, watching Riley with a stare that was both cold and compelling.

'No, sir. Absolutely not, sir,' Riley said at last, getting enough irony into his tone to make him feel good and the Superintendent to change tack. He turned to his desk, puzzled, fingers pressed to his pink temples. Riley left the window, sat opposite him like a good and chastened little policeman.

'I could of course take you off the case. Pressure, emotional involvement. It is, after all, only a routine investigation on the books. I could do that and if I thought it would help you . . . As you know, the powers that be, our task- and pay-masters are clamouring for more experienced men on the beat, community policing . . . I have a treble responsibility, you see, to you, to my men and to my masters—'

'I want to crack this one, sir. If I've stepped out of line at all, it's only because I'm so frustrated . . . '

The Superintendent quelled him with a look that turned into a slightly sneering smile. He did believe Riley was learning.

'Then find me a boy,' he said, hammering each word home. 'Find me the girl, her body, if you must, but don't, whatever you do, put me in difficult positions by leaning on helpless half-wits. Got it?'

'Yes, sir. Thank you very much, sir.'

Tait nodded. Riley stood up quickly, considered if he should say anything else, leave or wait to be dismissed.

'You will be familiar, of course, with procedures in incidents like this. However, I feel it my duty to remind you that anything written down in a report on an offending officer is subject to review, to revision, to put it simply, Riley, to *change* until it leaves this desk. Do you understand that?'

'Absolutely, sir.'

'I hope so.'

The nod, the tone were unequivocal. Riley went. Riley went quickly. He wanted a pint to wash the taste of a terrible day from his mouth. But first, instinct or malice or a simple hunch prompted him to do something he had neither the time nor the nerve to analyse. From a folder in a locked drawer in his office, he took two sharp photocopies of Karen Ashburton's drawing of Robert Luman, folded and slipped them into his breast pocket. He patted them, felt them safe against his heart. He knew a couple of people who would find the drawing very interesting, very useful, people who were always hungry for a leak. He made his escape to the pub, to lick his wounds.

SIX

Michael was drying and styling his hair.

It was what Buck had said in the pub last night that had made him decide to go to the police at last, after all. Buck was supposed to be his best mate but sometimes he behaved like a great wally. He knew Michael had been playing it cool, did not want his thing with Leni Mitchell to become public knowledge and yet there he'd been last night, prancing about the public bar, waving the evening paper over his head, drawing attention to himself and, by association, Michael.

'Why didn't you tell us?' Buck had said, leaning over Michael, a daft grin on his face.

'Tell you what?'

'You've not seen the *Post* then?'

'No.' Michael had tried to snatch it but Buck jumped away, nearly knocking some guy's pint flying. 'For Christ's sake sit down and behave.'

'Your guilty secret's out, mate. The truth is out,' he'd said, sliding along the bench until he was close to Michael, nudging him.

'What you on about?'

'She ditched you, didn't she? For a better-looking fellow.'

The paper lay now, folded in four, beside Michael's rumpled bed. He could see it, reflected in the tilted mirror and, for a moment, he switched off the hair-dryer and stared at it. Downstairs the washing machine thumped and juddered. Michael shrugged, flipped the comb back into his corn-blond hair and switched on the dryer.

Buck had gone off to the bar, sniggering, while Michael spread the paper flat on the table in front of him, smoothing the creases.

THE LAST MAN TO SEE LENORA ALIVE?

104

And below it, 'An artist's impression of a local man who, the *Post* can exclusively reveal, has been helping the police with their enquiries.' He was an ugly-looking sod, pathetic, not all there by the look of it. Buck's 'joke' stung. The blood had mounted to Michael's face and he realised that, for a moment, he'd been dead scared.

'You can see any bird'd drop you for him.'

'Shut it.'

Buck had slopped two half-pints onto the table.

'Oh yeah, a real Rambo, him.'

'I said, shut it or I'll—'

'OK, OK. Only joking.'

'Halves?'

'I'm short.'

'You're always bloody short.'

'I can't help it. It's not my fault.' Buck had stared at the picture. 'What d'you reckon, then?'

'Shut up and let us read.'

The short box of text which Michael had read again later, in the privacy of his own room, told him little. It was not until he had read it all through slowly and turned to page four, as bidden, where the now-familiar picture of Leni was reproduced with the question: *Have you seen this girl?* followed by the usual description, a rehash of the known facts and the extensive search of the area, the school precincts, that Michael was able to relax. He was not mentioned. It was mostly about how clever the *Post* was to get this picture and how the police had let the bloke go 'for technical reasons' and a lot of guff about greater police powers and 'the threat to public safety'. Michael had folded the paper up and drained his half-pint.

'Well?' Buck had nagged.

'Well what?'

'What d'you think?'

'Nothing.'

But he had thought about it a lot, later, and before falling asleep he had decided, definitely, to go to the police. He had woken with a sinking feeling, unable to remember at first what threatened to cloud his day. When he remembered his decision, he wavered for a moment, but then all the arguments came flooding back and he knew he had better get it over with. The longer he left it, the worse it would look for him. The picture gave him an excuse, had prompted something into his mind that he had not thought about since Leni went missing. The first time it seemed to him there was a possibility that something bad had happened to her. It made him feel funny and he concentrated more intently on his hair.

He had not gone to the police in the first place because it simply had not occurred to him. He knew Leni had gone off somewhere to sort herself out. That's what he'd told her to do. He wasn't going to blow the whistle on himself. There was a chance she might come back all right. He had nothing to gain by going to the police and he couldn't see how it would help her. If they wanted to know something, they ought to come asking. That was his philosophy. What had the police ever done for him? He shook his head, making the crest of blond curls tremble. He switched off the hair-dryer and, with his fingers, felt the tail of hair that hung between his shoulder blades. Anyway, he didn't want his private life splashed across the papers and neither would Leni. He'd just taken his City and Guilds at the tech and his tutor reckoned he'd do pretty well. In a couple of months he'd be in London, could really start to live. Meanwhile, the summer stretched lazily before him, a week on the Norfolk Broads with Buck and the gang, birds to pull . . . Michael smoothed the cropped fleece at the sides of his skull and tweaked at a curl which did not fall quite right onto his forehead. Then, satisfied, he stood up and pulled on a boat-necked white T-shirt, careful not to disarrange his hair. It clung to his narrow, muscular chest and he tugged it down so that it was moulded to his body. Pleased with himself, totally absorbed in the fashioning of his appearance, he sat down again, adjusted the mirror and leaned close to it. He began to apply a light coating of make-up, gold in colour, with a single black line under his lower lashes. Besides, there was the Passington Mr Disco competition. He did not want any adverse publicity until he'd got that sewn up. He had his heart set on it, had been practising every minute he got. He patted his face carefully with tissues, examined his image critically. He grinned at himself. Handsome bugger. Standing, he pulled on a pair of white, thigh-length shorts and fastened them. Sitting on the edge of the unmade bed, he added white, calf-high socks and a pair of white canvas shoes. He stood and turned to assess the effect in the mirror. This was difficult, required much twisting, turning and bending and he cursed, for the umpteenth time, the lack of a full-length mirror. He fitted his image together in pieces, decided that he would do.

The washing machine was silent as he went down the stairs, but Jimmy Young was prattling to someone about something.

'Is that you, Michael?'

'Yeah.'

'Where you going?'

'Out.'

And he went, slamming the door behind him.

Karen Ashburton parked her elderly Mini badly behind a glittering grey Volvo estate and sat, glaring ahead, her hands still clutching the wheel. She did not know how to begin, knew only that she had to try and had better get it over with quickly. As she was locking the car, Dr Bugler let herself out of the bungalow and stood for a moment, sniffing the air, the roses. Then she saw Karen and came, with a swinging stride that always made her look as though she was wearing wellington boots, down the path.

' 'Morning, Karen. Long time no see.'

'Hello, Doctor. Nothing wrong, I hope?'

'Nothing that won't mend. How are you? How's life at the tech?'

'Fine,' Karen said and surprised herself with the ease of the lie. Nothing was fine, everything was wrong. Tom was sure he was going to get the job at Breeton College and she felt it in her bones, or rather in her solar plexus, which ached dully at the thought of losing him. And there was this mess with the picture . . .

'You home for the hols?'

'Er . . . not really. I've got . . . work to do in Passington . . .'

'Well, don't forget to pop in and see your parents. I know they miss you.'

Karen knew that it was futile to be angry, that people like Dr Bugler, the elders of the village as she called them, would always see her and treat her as a child, telling her what to do and when to do it. Sometimes, she could even believe that they meant well.

'Doctor, is Mrs Luman in? Is it all right to go in?' she asked anxiously, delaying the woman, willing her to say, 'No, not now,' so that she could put it off for a while longer.

'Yes, I should think so. Probably be glad to see you. Needs cheering up. 'Bye, now.'

Karen watched the car draw away, the doctor waving and signalling in one windmill gesture from the window. Phyllis Luman would scarcely be glad to see her. Even if she didn't know or hadn't guessed, she would soon discover the extent of Karen's treachery. She could have sat down on the path right there and then and wept. Mrs Luman had always been so nice to her, so welcoming and uncritical and, in her early teens, Karen had grown really fond of Robert. She would never do anything, anything at all to hurt either of them. And now she had. And the consequences of it had to be faced. Karen drew herself up, took a deep, deep breath to steady herself and held it until she reached the front door and heard the muffled buzz of the bell.

The extent of the damage she had caused stared accusingly out at her from Phyllis Luman's face; she had aged ten years. Her eyes had a restless, hunted expression, seemed to haunt the space behind Karen. She clutched a quilted pink housecoat to her throat as though she feared an assault. Slowly her eyes came to rest, softened.

'Oh, hello, Karen.'

'Hello, Mrs Luman. Sorry to call . . . like this,' she added feebly, realising that it was neither early nor could she know –

though she could fear – the reason for Dr Bugler's visit. 'Can you spare me a minute? It's important. I've got to talk to you.'

'Of course, dear. You know I'm always glad to see you. Come in.' She left the door, seemed to drift towards the sitting room. Karen stepped into the hall, wiped her sandalled feet thoroughly and unnecessarily out of nervousness.

She had never seen the sitting room so untidy. Cups stood about unwashed. The *Passington Post* glared up at her from the arm of the settee. Fortunately it was face down, the drawing of Robert hidden. But not for long, Karen thought. This was not a reprieve, just a temporary, agonising stay of execution.

Phyllis Luman sat in her customary chair, as though exhausted, and pulled the skirt of her housecoat around her.

'Are you all right?' Karen asked anxiously, dropping her shoulder bag onto the floor and sitting in Paula Brownlow's chair. 'Can I get you anything?'

'No, dear, thank you. I'm all right. I've just had a bad night. A lot of bad nights lately. It's Robert. You probably saw the doctor . . . '

'It's about Robert . . . '

'I expect you've heard. Well, everyone must know by now. He was so upset. I've never seen him like that, not for years, anyway. I had to give him one of his special pills – you remember?' Karen nodded quickly. 'It didn't seem to do any good, though. I suppose he was too worked up. I couldn't persuade him to take another one. I just couldn't. He's too strong for me. I had to send for Dr Bugler. She's wonderful. She came out last night and now again this morning. She's put him to sleep. She says it's for the best but I don't know . . . '

'I'm so sorry,' Karen said, tears filling her eyes. 'Honest. I don't know how to apologise . . . '

'Apologise? Whatever for, dear?'

'The picture. There, in the paper . . . ' Karen pointed.

Phyllis turned her head slowly and looked at the newspaper. Loathing and resignation, Karen thought, passed across her face, then anger, a righteous and justified anger.

'That!' She spat the word. 'If I could only lay my hands on . . . '

109

'It was me,' Karen said, feeling that the world was about to collapse around her. 'It's all my fault, and I'm so terribly, dreadfully sorry.'

'You? But why would you . . . ? Oh, Karen, no. You were always so good with Robert. How could you?'

'It was all a mistake, an accident . . .'

'To let them print a picture . . . Oh, *you* drew it. Of course . . .'

'I didn't let them print it. I don't know who did that. I told them it was all a mistake . . .'

'I'm sorry, Karen. I don't understand. I don't understand how you could.'

'Let me explain, please. Then I'll go and never bother you again.'

Phyllis Luman folded her hands in her lap but could not keep them still. They twisted and knotted, laced and unlaced there as though out of her control. The nod of her head, permitting Karen to speak, was defeated. Karen explained, as quickly and simply as she could, how she had come to make the drawing, how she had told Riley it was a mistake. At the mention of his name a sort of flinch tightened the muscles around Phyllis Luman's mouth, drawing her lips into a straight, hard line.

'But I don't know how it got into the papers. The police must have done that. They wouldn't let me have my drawing back. Oh I should have warned you . . . I thought the Superintendent believed me. He seemed sympathetic . . . It just goes to show you should never, ever trust the police.'

'That's enough, Karen.' Phyllis put her left hand to her forehead, gently massaged her temple, her face turned away from Karen.

'I'm so dreadfully sorry. I wanted to tell you that. I swear I never . . . I would never, not knowingly, do anything to hurt Robert. I don't expect you'll believe me . . . How could you . . . ?'

'Don't be silly, dear. It's not your fault.'

'But it is. You haven't been listening.'

'You don't understand. The girl, she identified him, and the bus driver. Robert was there that day, in Passington anyway. He might have seen the missing girl . . . So you see it's not your fault at all. The police were bound to question him. They had no choice.'

Karen could not believe it. She had convinced herself so thoroughly of her own guilt, had cast herself so convincingly as the traitor and bringer of all ills that she could not relinquish the role, did not, in part, want it taken away from her.

'No,' she argued. 'If I hadn't made that drawing—'

'I already knew. I found the bus ticket in his pocket. I was on my way to see Constable Smith with Mr June when the police came. It really isn't your fault.'

'But I told them that I knew Robert, where he lived. I thought they'd understand then . . . '

'They would have found him anyway. I was going to tell them. I didn't have any choice.'

'Oh God,' Karen said.

The silence was bleak. Karen could only stare at Mrs Luman's hands. Mrs Luman herself seemed lost, beyond reach.

'What's going to happen now?' Karen asked at last.

Phyllis Luman shook her head.

'I don't know. Robert can't tell them anything.' She grew angry, defensive. 'They can only put words in his mouth. They upset him so dreadfully. Mr June says I must see a solicitor, but I don't know . . . '

'Of course you must. You must protect Robert. Robert wouldn't harm a fly.'

Phyllis Luman's eyes fastened on her face, demanding, searching it. Karen, her heart skipping, saw hope brighten in them.

'You really mean that, Karen? You do, don't you? You're not just—'

'Of course. I mean, I know Robert. You know I do. You must remember how I used to take him to Lulford for picnics, walks? Robert was always as gentle as a lamb.'

'Oh you don't know how good it is to hear you say that.'

'You mustn't let them put ideas into your head,' Karen said.

111

'They're bastards, the police, all of them.'

'Oh no, dear, you mustn't say that. Mr Jolley, the Superintendent, they were ever so nice. And, after all, they did have to question him. It was their duty—'

'Don't you let them near him again. You get a good solicitor. My father would help, I'm sure . . . '

'Perhaps you're right.'

'I know I am.'

'I just hope and pray that poor girl will turn up somewhere soon, safe and sound . . . '

'Perhaps she will,' Karen said, but it didn't feel right or likely. 'Anyway, thank you for seeing me, being so nice.'

'It was very brave of you to come,' Phyllis said, 'but I don't want any more talk of it all being your fault. You have nothing to blame yourself for. Nothing.' Phyllis Luman stood up. 'And, you know, Robert loves the picture. Mr Jolley let him have a copy. He thinks it's wonderful. He'll be so pleased to know—'

'Do you have to tell him? I'd rather he didn't know.'

Phyllis looked at her, puzzled. Then she picked up the paper, turned it over, stared at the picture.

'It really is very good. You've caught him just so.'

'It's wicked, publishing it like that. You know how people talk, gossip. I wish there was something I could do.'

'Thank you, Karen, but it's out of our hands now. We can only wait and see.'

'There might be reporters, you know, calling at the house.'

'Oh I don't think so, dear. I expect it'll all be a seven-days wonder.' She dropped the paper onto the occasional table. 'It's Robert I worry about. He was so upset at the police station.'

'Perhaps I could . . . ' She had been going to offer to take him out, over to Lulford, perhaps, for a walk in the country park, but she bit the offer back. It would be asking for trouble to take Robert anywhere at the moment. 'I wish I could do something,' she repeated. 'Perhaps I could come and talk to him, when he's . . . better.'

'Actually,' Phyllis said suddenly, her face brightening, 'there is something, if you had the time. I can tell you. You'll understand.'

'What?' Karen demanded, immediately excited, her conscience still longing to be appeased.

'Well, the last couple of years he's become fascinated by those American comics. You know, Superman and all that sort of thing. It's silly, I know but . . . Anyway, he's set his heart on a sort of Superman outfit. You know how he is. Only he wants it different, something especially for him. It would have to have a hood, something to cover his poor head, you see.'

'Yes?'

'Well, I don't really know . . . You were always so good with your needle. I remember the lovely dresses you used to make . . . ' Phyllis was searching through a pile of magazines and papers, the *Radio Times*. 'Here,' she said and pulled out a comic. 'Something like this. It's the one thing I really think might make him forget . . . Help him to calm down. He's easily distracted, bless him.'

'I could design him one,' Karen said. 'I'd love to.'

'I don't want to put you to too much trouble . . . '

'It's easy. I'd like to. You don't know what a weight you've lifted from my mind.'

'I'd pay, of course. It's just that I – I don't feel up to needle-work much just now. I don't seem able to settle. And I never was a dressmaker. Knitting's more in my line.'

'Oh please let me do it. It'd be great, really, and if it makes up to Robert . . . '

'You're a good girl, Karen. It would be such a comfort to him. And me.'

'Have you got his measurements?'

'Yes, somewhere . . . '

'I'll get on with it straight away if you can find them.'

'Thank you, dear. Thank you so much. In my workbox I think.' Karen helped her find it, took the neat square of paper with Robert's measurements inscribed upon it. 'I always keep them by me, having to buy all his clothes and everything. He'll never stand still for anyone else.'

113

'I'll make him a real bobby-dazzler, just you wait and see.'
'Oh, he will be pleased. Really he will.'

The boy ambled into Riley's office, hands stuck nonchalantly into the pockets of his shorts, his face wearing a fixed expression of indifference and boredom. Riley looked him up and down. He was tall, probably over six feet, and slim as a rake, but not puny-looking. His hair and his clothes were the most startling thing about him. The sides of his head were shaved, not bald, but to a smooth, golden fleece that, in Riley's day, would have been called a crew cut. The top of his head, in contrast, bore a thick crest or mane of blond curls, like a punk Mohican without the spikes. It fell onto his forehead, like a curled horse's fringe, and down his back. All his clothing, what little there was of it, was pristine white and fitted him like the proverbial glove. He stood there, hands in his pockets, looking down at Riley who saw no advantage in standing up; the kid would still tower over him.

'You want to see me?'
'If you're the bloke in charge of the Leni Mitchell case, yeah.'
'Name?'
'Are you?'
'Yes. Name?'
'Michael Stones.'
'Address?'
'What for? I'm here, aren't I?'
'You want to talk to me, you give your name and address.'
'Twenty-three Mandela Drive.'
Riley wrote it down.
'So? What do you want?'
'I've got information. Might be useful. About Leni.'
'You knew Leni?'
'Yeah.'
'Girlfriend?'
'Yeah.'
'Then why the hell didn't you come forward sooner?'
Michael shrugged, looked around the room.
'Can I have a pew?'

114

Riley nodded towards a chair that stood against the wall. Laconically, Michael lifted it, set it before Riley's desk and sat. Sitting down he looked ungainly, his bony knees sticking up. He looked uncomfortable.

Luman's picture in the paper had been an inspired shot. It was bringing them crawling out of the woodwork. Last night, holding his breath with excitement, he'd seen one Stella Lambert in the presence of her concerned and prepared-to-be-stroppy father. Stella Lambert, a plain girl with unnaturally frizzy hair that did not become her, remembered seeing a man 'just like' Luman on her way from the main building of Passington Upper School to the town swimming pool. He had been walking along the road, pressed himself against the stone wall to let her pass. He had smiled at her 'sort of funny' and she had hurried to catch up her friends. Brilliant, Riley had thought, just the break he needed, except that the friends did not remember the incident at all and the girl could not be sure of the date. End of term and the timetable all to pot because of exams, kids being sent off hither and yon . . . Stella Lambert was a good swimmer, might even reach county standard. They had let her have a lot of extra coaching at the end of term with the result that no one could say for sure which day she saw Luman.

Riley swallowed his disappointment for the hundredth time and looked at Michael Stones, his unlikely but possible saviour.

'Right, now, what do you know?'

'Nothing much. It's just I saw that picture in the *Post* last night . . . '

Riley leaned forward eagerly.

'You recognised him?'

'No. Never seen him before. But it – like – it jogged my memory. Leni said there'd been some wally watching her, from the road. Laughing, she said, and she ran.'

'Hang on. When was this? And where?'

'Outside the school. That day. Wednesday, wasn't it? When she went missing, like.'

'You saw Leni after she left the school?'

115

'Yeah. She was coming to meet me, wasn't she?'

'Hold it right there.' Riley stood up, almost ran around the desk and opened the door. 'Jennings?' he bellowed. 'Bring your book and get in here quick.' He closed the door again, a flicker of excitement interfering with his breathing. 'You're going to make a statement,' he told Michael, returning to his desk. The boy looked up from a detailed study of his fingernails. With a start, Riley realised that what he had taken for the flawless complexion of youth was a discreet film of make-up and, now that he recognised it, he could smell it, slightly sweet on the air. The kid smelled like a cheap tart, he thought, and looked like something off *Top of the Pops*.

'Sure,' Michael said, tucking his hands under the backs of his thighs. 'That's what I came here for, isn't it?'

Jennings came in then, juggling book and pen.

'Mr Stones is going to make a statement. Get it down,' Riley said. 'Now, you'd known Lenora Mitchell how long?'

'Oh, I dunno . . . A few months. Six months, maybe. I met her at O'Grady's.' When he saw that this meant nothing to Riley, he added, 'The disco on Sheep Street.'

'I know it, sir,' Jennings put in.

'And?' Riley said, ignoring the constable.

'We danced, chatted. I asked her out.'

'You went out with her regularly?'

'Yeah. Two or three times a week, maybe. You know.'

'Were you sleeping with her?'

'Of course.' He looked and sounded truly surprised as though any other basis for a relationship between himself and a girl was unthinkable.

'You were serious, then?'

'Don't know what you mean.'

'Did you think of marrying her?'

'God, no. It was just . . . you know.'

'A casual sexual relationship?' Riley suggested.

'Yeah. I suppose.'

'All right. So what happened that morning?'

'Oh, yeah, right. Well, it was the night before, really. I didn't

116

see her. I was revising for my City and Guilds at the tech. I had two exams that Wednesday. Leni rang me, said she had to see me. I said, no way. She knew my City and Guilds were really important to me, but she went on and on, so I said, OK, I'd see her about half eleven. I thought that'd put her off, you know? But she said OK. She said she'd bunk off school. So I thought, well, it's her head, not mine. My first exam was over at eleven, see, and then I had a break until two and Mr Jones, my tutor, he says never to cram just before an exam. Just hang loose, stay cool.'

'Good for Mr Jones. So where did you arrange to meet her?'

'Down by the river. You know.'

'Where, exactly?'

'Well, it's difficult. You know that field in front of the school?' Riley nodded. 'There's a little wood at the bottom, right?' Again Riley nodded. 'And if you go through the wood – well, it's not really a wood, is it, more like a sort of copse . . . ?'

'I know the place.'

'Yeah, right. Well, you lot have searched there, haven't you?'

'Get on with it, Stones.'

'All right. Well, if you walk through the trees, like, from the field, you come out onto the river bank, don't you? I said I'd see her there. Half eleven.'

'How did you get there?'

'Walked, didn't I?'

'From the tech?'

'Yeah. Straight along the river. Come on, you must know it. Takes about what – ten, fifteen minutes?'

'So you got there early?'

'No. Why?'

'Because if your exam finished at eleven and it only takes fifteen minutes . . . '

'Oh, I get you. No. I hate being early, hate hanging around. I had a cup of coffee first. Then I sloped off around eleven fifteen.'

'Did you have coffee with anyone?'

'Yeah.'

'Who?'

Michael shifted in his chair, pulled his hands out from under him and folded one long leg over the other, smoothing his sock.

'Do I have to?'

'If you don't want to get in more trouble than you are already, yes.'

'OK.' He frowned. 'There was Buck. We call him that. John Buck. Chas Leary. Tommy – I can't say his other name. He's Cypriot or something. And Roxanne. Roxanne Kettle.'

'And after you'd had coffee with these people . . . ' Riley said, glancing at Jennings to make sure he'd got the names down.

'Pepsi, actually. I just remembered.'

'Pepsi, then. What?'

'I told you. I went along the towpath – that's what they call it, isn't it? Towpath, right. Went along there to the wood.'

'Did you see anyone?'

He shrugged again.

'I don't know.'

'It's important.'

'I must've done. I don't know. Yes. There was a couple of blokes fishing now I come to think about it. A red car.'

'On the towpath?' Riley said in disbelief.

'No. Parked up where the road comes down. Parson's Field, don't they call it? You know.'

Riley nodded.

'What sort of car?'

'Red.'

'Make?'

'Look, I don't know. I'm not into cars, OK? It wasn't a Roller, that's for sure.'

'Well, I expect someone will remember you,' Riley said drily.

'Yeah. 'Spect so.'

'Fishermen, you say?'

'Yeah. I think. I didn't take much notice.'

'You didn't pass anyone, speak to anyone? No one asked you the time or . . . '

'No. I never spoke to no one. I might have passed someone. I don't remember. All I remember is the red car. And a couple of blokes fishing.'

'Together?'

'Might have been. I don't know.'

'Were they sitting or standing together?'

'No. Separate. Miles apart.'

'All right. Then you met Leni.'

'No. Not straight off. When I got to the wood she wasn't there, so I goes through the other side and seen her coming towards me across the field.'

'Then what?'

'I went to meet her.'

'And?'

'She said she'd fallen, climbing the wall. The field drops down, you know. That's when she told me about the bloke, this wally.'

'What did she tell you?'

'That he'd watched her and burst out laughing when she fell. She said she gave him the V sign. Know what I mean?'

'Yes.'

'She was upset, mad, you know. About the fall and him laughing, so I told her to forget it. I put my arm around her and we went into the wood.'

'You didn't see this man?'

'No. She pointed to where he'd been but I didn't really look. I was trying to calm her down. And I wasn't going to stand out there in the middle of a field, right in front of her school with her playing hookey, was I?'

'So you went into the wood?'

'Right.'

'And?'

'She tells me she's pregnant.'

'You were surprised?'

'Yes.'

'Why?'

'I thought she was on the pill, didn't I?'

'You didn't take precautions?'

''Course not.' He sounded affronted, as though such a practice was beneath him, strictly for the wallies.

'You were the father?'

'I never said that. That's what she . . . what she wanted me to think.'

'Did you say you weren't?'

'No. It never came up.'

'So, let's just see if I've got this right. Leni tells you she's pregnant and you . . . you said, what?'

'Oh. I said, "Oh", I think. I didn't know what to say. Then she said, "What are we going to do about it?" and I said, "I don't know. Don't ask me." Something like that.'

'That must have been a great comfort to her . . . '

'No. I don't think so. She kept on crying, anyway. Oh, I see what you— Very funny.'

'She was crying?'

'Yeah. So I said, well, she'd have to do something about it.'

'Meaning what?'

'Get it fixed. Abortion.'

'What did Leni say?'

'She never said nothing. She was just crying.'

'And all the time, at the back of your mind, was the possibility that you weren't the father. Right?'

Michael considered this, weighed it. He put his leg down to the floor, sat up straighter, hands resting on his bare knees.

'Look, I'm not saying Leni was a slag. All I know is, I wasn't the first. She'd done it before. Before doing it with me, I mean. I wasn't the first. So . . . ' He shrugged again. 'Anyway, that wasn't the point. I could've been the father. Easy. I don't deny that. But I wasn't about to do anything about it. I mean, what could I do? I'm a student. I certainly wasn't going to marry her.'

'Did you tell her that?'

'No. We never discussed anything like that. All I said was, hadn't she got an auntie somewhere she could go to and stay with? That's what they do, isn't it? And get it fixed. After all, it was nearly the school holidays. She could bugger off for a bit and get it fixed and nobody'd be any the wiser. See?'

'I see. Did Leni?'

'Well, she calmed down after a bit. She said she had an aunt in Manchester. I said, "Right. That's it then." Or something like that. She said she'd have to talk to her mum first and I said that was a good idea.'

'And then what?'

'What?'

'You just left it there? That was it?'

'Yeah. Sort of.'

'Listen, if you don't tell me everything . . . '

'I am. I'm going to. I know what you're thinking. That's why I'm going to tell you everything.'

'Fine. Good. So let's get on with it.'

'Well, like I said, that's how we left it. She'd talk to her mum and go to her auntie in Manchester and get it fixed. Then I had her.'

'What?' Riley looked at him, unable to conceal his astonishment.

'I had her. We did it. You know—'

'You mean to say you . . . had intercourse with her . . . there and then?'

'Yeah. There was no one about. And it was a bit late to worry about the consequences, wasn't it?'

They're animals, Riley thought. Just bloody animals, perpetually in rut.

'Have you got that, Jennings?' he asked.

'Yes, sir.'

'Then what?'

'I went back to the tech.'

'You just left her?'

'Well, I couldn't take her with me, could I? I'd got an exam at two.'

'Right. You just left her.'

'Not like that. I said, "Cheerio," kissed her and that. I told her to take the afternoon off, tell her mum like we'd

121

agreed. She said "OK," and off I went.'

'What time was that?'

'Don't know.'

'You went straight back to college?'

'Sure.'

'You see anyone there?'

'Yeah. I met up with Buck and some of the others in the canteen. They can tell you.'

'What time would that be?'

'One? Quarter past? I don't know.'

'And then?'

'I sat my exam.'

'And you haven't seen her since?'

'No.'

'Heard from her?'

'No.'

'And you did nothing.'

'Ah, well, I knew you'd say that. I thought she'd done it, see. I thought she'd taken my advice and gone to Manchester.'

'Don't you read the papers?'

'Not much.'

'You read it last night.'

'Someone pointed it out to me, that picture, like.'

'You didn't know she was missing?'

'Well, yes, but I thought, like I said, I just thought she'd gone to her auntie's.'

'To get an abortion and let you off the hook?'

'I wasn't on any hook. Like I told you, I wasn't going to do anything. She knew the risks she was taking. I never forced her. She was willing enough. Like I said, I wasn't the first. So what could I do?'

'You could have taken care of her.'

'How? With what?'

Riley conceded there was no answer to that and no point in talking to the likes of Michael Stones about compassion and emotional support.

'You realise that you were probably the last person to see Leni?'

'I might have been. I don't know.'

'What's more, you are probably the last person to have seen her alive.'

'Oh, now we're getting to it. Fine. You write this down,' he said to Jennings. ' "I didn't kill Leni. She was alive when I left her. Alive and well." '

'And pregnant.'

'So she said.'

'And who said she's dead?' That stopped him. Riley felt a kind of pleasure as, for the first time since he had entered the room, Michael Stones's indifferent, callous confidence cracked. The make-up looked stark on his suddenly pale face. The cords in his slim, elegant neck stood out as he swallowed.

'You did. That's what you think,' he said at last. 'You said I was probably the last—'

'And it didn't come as a bit of shock to you, did it? Right, Jennings. Have someone take him down and get that typed up. As for you,' he leaned across the desk, towards Michael, 'you better prepare yourself for a charge.'

'Of what? Like I said, nobody knows she's dead, if she's dead.'

'I can have you for withholding information any time I like. And by the time I've been through your cock and bull story and had it checked, I'll be able to nail you.'

'Never. I never did anything, except for what I've told you. I only came here because I reckoned you ought to get after that bloke, the one in the paper—'

'We've already got him,' Riley said, smiling. 'And now we've got you as well.' He went to the door and opened it. 'All right, Jennings. Get on with it.'

The old man had told him to find a boy and a boy, feeling he was safe but carrying a bad conscience, had fallen straight into his lap. That report, about his questioning of Luman would end up precisely where it belonged, in the waste-paper basket. And the cherry on the cake was that he would enjoy breaking Michael Stones down. He wanted to see him cry, like poor, pregnant Leni had cried, before, as he so graphically put it, he had had her. By the time Riley finished with him, he'd wish he'd never learned what it was for.

The inside of Robert's head felt soft and white from the many pricks the doctor-lady had given him. It was not a nice soft like the wool of his blue hat or a remembered teddy bear. It made him groan when he sat up. He knew where he was, of course, but outside of that was a yawning void of memory, blank white walls which, like canvas, yielded to and yet escaped the touch. Robert shouted.

'Mam. Mam.'

He began the laborious business of exchanging pyjamas for day clothes. Each movement, every stretch and bend seemed to happen in slow motion, to take too long. He gave up, settled for an amalgamation of clothes, wearing his V-neck sweater back to front. He went into the kitchen but there was no smell of breakfast. He drank a lot of water for his throat was parched. For a long time, fighting his soft brain, he studied the electric kettle, the tea caddy, the pot. They formed a trinity, he knew, but one which would not fit together in the right order. Impatient with himself, angry, he blundered out of the kitchen into the sitting room, calling, 'Mam, Mam, Mam,' and went again into the hall, back into his room. He needed a ciggie, took one and lit it with a wavering hand. He coughed and dragged eagerly, blowing out smoke, until only a beige butt remained, began to smoulder and smell. He went out again, turned to his mother's room and saw her then through the half-open door. She was sleeping, lying on top of the bed in her pink housecoat, looking very peaceful. Reassured by the sight of her, Robert leaned in the doorway, smiling and dribbling. There was a small vial of pills on the nightstand beside her. Robert dashed the dribble away and wiped his hand on his pyjama trousers. On elaborate tiptoes he backed into the hall saying, 'Ssh, ssh,' to himself, holding a finger in front of his mouth. The tip of his finger made him go cross-eyed and for a moment there was two of everything, two telephones and two tables, two doors into the sitting room which slid together and became one as he shouldered it aside.

Robert fumbled around the room, found a mug half-full of cold coffee and stared at it, considered drinking it but did not like the skin of milk that clung to the side of the mug when he tilted it. He put it down and switched on the television, sat impatiently on the settee, tapping his feet, waiting for the slow picture to come up. When it did he growled at it. White men moving slowly and mysteriously, a long arcing shot of blue sky. Robert got down on his hands and knees and scuttled clumsily about the room, rearing up to search chair seats and other surfaces for the remote-control handset. He could not find it. He pretended to be a dog, sniffing it out, but became bored. He sighed heavily and pulled himself upright, returned, with a plodding step, to his seat. Robert did not like cricket. He could never see the ball, did not understand its abstruse rules. He stared at the picture, humming to himself, tapping his feet, tapping his hands on his knees in a counter-rhythm. In time, he knew, the cricket would go away. He set himself to wait but the disconnected diving, running, throwing movements of the men in white could not hold his attention. He looked around the room, narrowing his field of vision with each exaggerated sweep of his head until his eye struck against the newspaper draped over the arm of the settee. He snatched it to him, stared at the back page with its columns of black figures and its picture of a white man waving a cricket bat in the air.

Robert could read well, far beyond the 'pows' and 'zaps' of his beloved comic books but, as several doctors had pointed out, what connections the words made in his mind, how much he could be said to understand what he read, no one could know. Unable to give the information back with any verbal coherence, it remained a matter of speculation whether Robert read and understood as any other person might but was doomed to keep the information for ever to himself, or if the words made some pattern and picture known only to him.

He read his way doggedly through the small ads, crying out with recognition at the letters 'ET', trying to share his excitement with the empty room.

'ET,' he said and grinned and turned the pages.

Robert found the picture of Leni Mitchell. He did not like it, associated it with bad feelings but it held his attention for some time and, underlining the print with his finger, he read the paragraph below the picture. 'Missing' meant 'gone' meant 'gone to Heaven' meant 'dead'. Like Dad. He liked 'hunt' and 'search'. He giggled at 'increasing alarm', and 'fear for safety'. He read the whole piece again, sensing in it some importance, some connection with himself that excited him. He lifted his eyes from the paper, frowned at the television screen, his eyes narrowed so that the white men became blurred and misty like creatures in a fog. The girl's face formed out of this fog, flushed and turned to him. He saw her tumbling, falling down, her skirt thrown up and

'Knickers!' he said and spluttered with suppressed laughter.

The girl scrambled to her feet, brushing at her skirt and looked up at him with Riley's face, twisted in that fierce, awful way.

'No,' Robert shouted and, with an uncoordinated movement, flung the paper in his lap to the floor where it fell closed, his own picture staring up at him. Robert tried to stare himself down but he lost. He got onto his hands and knees again, stooped over his own image. 'Robert,' he said and louder, 'Robert.'

Well done, Robert!

Pleased, Robert read the text in the box below his picture. Many of the phrases were familiar from the television, from programmes he particularly liked where cars chased cars and crashed and burst into flames. 'Helping the police with their enquiries'. 'Released'. 'One of the last people to see Lenora Mitchell, alive or dead'.

Robert was sucked back into the police station, the questions echoing in his head. He did not like this but it held a certain fascination for him. He felt as though he was making his way along some dark corridor, slapping his hands against its solid walls sure that he could emerge at the end into some light, into

126

some clear knowledge. Whatever it was, it eluded him. The tunnel closed and resolved itself into his black and white face staring up at him from the newspaper.

It burst on Robert then, in Robert, like a flower opening, petal by petal, each one stretching and taking on its full and proper shape until it hung whole and perfect in the sunlight. At the foot of the page, in a box headed *In tomorrow's Post* was a picture of Shakin' Stevens. Scrabbling at the paper, creasing and almost tearing it, Robert turned the pages excitedly, saw Prince Charles and a man he did not know opening something and the nice lady Mam liked who read the local news on TV, who had long yellow hair made dull grey by the newspaper's printing. Robert added it up. All these people – Shakin' Stevens and Prince Charles and the man he did not know and the newsreader – all of them were famous. Only famous people got their pictures in the paper. Robert turned carefully, almost reverentially back to the front page, to his own likeness.

Well done, Robert!

Sammy had been a pest all afternoon, yelling and screaming and throwing his toys out of the playpen, then screaming until she picked them up for him. He slept now, fitfully, red-faced and clutching a Galt yellow engine to his chest. Di Smith, his mother, was also red-faced, with exertion and the fury she felt towards this child, the overflowing basket of ironing and from the damp heat of the steam iron itself. She searched half-heartedly through the basket, looking for Arthur's shirt, the one he would expect, clean and pressed and ready for tomorrow morning, and wanted to burst into tears when two Babygros and her own pink blouse fell to the floor. The doorbell shrilling was the last straw. But she had to answer, not just because it was her strict duty when Arthur was out, but also because she feared it would wake the baby. She fought her way through the cluttered living room, into which the front door immediately opened, and saw it, for a moment, with Arthur's jaded, disappointed eyes. She had not even drawn the curtains properly and the tray with the remains of Arthur's supper was still balanced on the arm of the settee.

'Yes?' she snapped, holding the door half-open. She did not, for a moment, recognise him and then a whole package of knowledge and associations flooded her mind, alerting her and making her instinctively afraid.

'Police,' he said.

'He's not here. You can't see him now.'

'Yes.'

He lifted up a copy of last night's *Post*, crumpled and with the newsprint smudged by much handling and jabbed a finger at his own image, grinning broadly.

'Help police,' he said.

'Well, you can't help them now. Constable Smith—'

'Yes,' he said loudly. 'Now.'

'No. You don't understand . . . '

He pushed the door with the whole of his left arm, not with so very much force but taking Di Smith by surprise. The door was snatched from her grasp and Robert Luman stepped inside.

'You can't—' She stopped herself, got her anger under control. Firstly, he was supposed to be harmless, just a bit do-lally. She had nodded and smiled at his mother, been reassured about him by other young women in the village. Secondly, she had been warned about and trained for just such an emergency. If anything ever happens, Arthur had always added, just stay calm, act as natural as you can and keep talking. She backed into the room, by luck avoiding Sammy's scattered toys, the clutter. He swung his head, a bit like an uncertain animal, she thought. 'You can wait,' she said quickly. 'He won't be long. He's due back at any minute. Have you got the right time on you?' She half-turned away from him, picked up the tray and held it, like a barrier or a potential weapon between her body and his. 'Why don't you sit down here? I'm sure he won't be long. In fact, I'm expecting him at any minute.' On the other hand he had been questioned by the Passington CID and Arthur said there was something up, something they weren't saying. Thank God, he had not closed the front door. She looked out through it longingly. 'Please sit down.' She moved

128

aside so that he could get to the sofa. Her legs wanted to make a dash for it. She could see herself already on the path, nearing the gate, screaming her head off. Then she remembered Sammy. He sat. Oh thank God, he sat down. Di Smith hurried towards the kitchen. 'Would you like the television on? A cup of tea, perhaps . . . ' She got through the door, into the steamy atmosphere of the kitchen and clattered the tray, cup and plate and all into the sink. Sammy lay on his side, safe, sucking his thumb.

'Tea,' he said, startling her.

'You go and sit down then and I'll bring you one. It won't take a minute.'

'Baby.'

'Yes, baby.' She went to the playpen and placed herself squarely between him and Robert Luman. 'You're Robert Luman, aren't you? I've seen you around. I know your mother. Just to speak to, you know. How is she? Why don't you go and sit down and I'll—'

'Famous,' he said. 'Robert Luman.'

'Oh, the *famous* Robert Luman, are you? Yes, of course. Well, that's nice.'

He nodded, smiling and brought the newspaper up close to his eyes. After a moment he began to move away from the door, back towards the settee. She waited until he had sat down and then filled the kettle, looking over her shoulder nervously.

He told Arthur Smith and Mrs Arthur Smith made him a cup of tea. It was good tea. He liked Mrs Arthur Smith because she called him famous Robert Luman. He liked the baby, too, who squeaked and wriggled in Mrs Arthur's arms. When Arthur Smith went to telephone about him, Mrs Arthur stood clutching the baby to her, watching him. Robert got down on the floor and pushed a red truck of bricks about. He was still doing this, quite happy and absorbed, when Paula Brownlow arrived and shouted at him to get up and stop making a spectacle of himself.

Paula took him home, prodding him in the small of the back, trying to take his arm. He slapped her away.

129

'Look at you. Look at the state of you. Pyjama trousers, sweater on back to front. What do you want a sweater for on a hot day like this, anyway? Eh?'

'Famous,' he shouted belligerently and pushed her away.

'I'll give you famous, my boy. I'll have you put away if it's the last thing I do.'

He ran away from her when they reached the gate, turned to look at her, all flushed and with her blonde hair coming down. Then Mam was at the door, clutching at him and crying.

''S'all right. 'S'all right,' he told her. 'Robert famous.' Then he realised he had lost the paper and went lurching back down the path in search of it.

'Oh no you don't. Get inside this minute. Go on.' Paula barred his way, her arms waving and thrashing at the air. 'This instant,' she yelled.

'It's all right, dear. Come along. Mam's here.'

'That boy'll be the death of you,' Paula shouted as, suddenly docile and hanging his head, Robert turned at his mother's pressure on his arm and went towards the front door. 'You mark my words.'

'Please, Paula. It was my fault. I shouldn't have taken that pill.'

'Pill? You'll need more than pills. You'll be in a padded cell before him if this goes on.' Paula slammed the door behind her, shook her head in exasperation as Phyllis led him into his room, talking softly, soothing him.

'Are you, dear? That's nice. I always knew you would be one day.'

'Mad,' Paula muttered. 'She's getting as bad as him.' Something would have to be done. Paula vowed it. She would see to it. Tucking in the stray wisps of her hair, Paula stomped off to put the kettle on.

Di Smith was still frightened, still held Sammy clutched tightly in her arms. He struggled and began to yell, wanting to get down but she could not bear to part with him, not yet. Arthur, standing at the wall phone waved her away, covered his left ear, but she could not leave him either. Through the open kitchen door she could see the red truck, its multicoloured building bricks where Robert Luman had left it on the floor.

'A bit upset, sir. Yes, sir. I don't know, sir. It's hard to say. Well, sir, if it was anyone else, well, you might say it amounted to a confession, sir.'

'A confession?' Jolley tensed in his seat and pressed the telephone closer to his ear.

'Well, that could be an interpretation, sir. I mean, if he was normal, like.'

'Did he seem upset?'

'No, sir. Quite cheerful. His normal self, you might say, if he was—'

'Yes, yes. So what did he say?'

'Well, just words, sir, really. Kept on about "famous" and, "I did it." I tried to ask him, you know, sir, the usual sort of questions, where, when and how, that sort of thing, but, well, sir, to be honest I don't think he had a bloody clue.'

'All right, Smith. You did well to call me. File a report to me personally . . . '

'I wondered if I should ring Passington, sir?'

'No. Leave that to me. Leave everything to me, but let me have a full report, no matter how daffy it may sound. Got that?'

'Yes, sir. Will do, sir.'

'Any chance of it tonight?'

'Oh, I don't know, sir. I'll give it a try, sir.'

'Good man. And I'm sorry your missus was upset. Tell her from me, will you?'

'Yes, sir. Thank you, sir.'

He hung up shaking his head.

'Oh, I was so scared,' Di said over the baby's yells. Arthur Smith went to her and folded his arms around her. Sammy, squashed between them, gurgled happily and pressed his hot, wet face against his father's. 'What if he did?' Di said. 'What if, in his own way, he was telling the truth?'

'I don't know, love. I just don't know,' Arthur said sadly.

SEVEN

She was becoming an encumbrance and time was running out.

Kerry Mather looked at her where she stood, propped up and swathed in grey plastic in one half of the wardrobe. With a sweep of his left arm, he opened the corresponding door and looked at his clothes, all squashed up tight together now, not spaced out equidistantly, with a pungent Mothak hung in every alternate space. Two pairs of winter cords, an old pair of flannels, his spare jeans. One tweed sports jacket, one navy-blue blazer which he never wore, two bomber jackets, his one good suit, kept pressed and cleaned and ready for the next interview, the hoped-for, elusive job. A pair of white cotton trousers, an impulse purchase hardly ever worn because his mother condemned them as impractical. He put out his right hand to touch them and automatically began to arrange his clothes along the bar, according to training and custom. The back of his hand, his wrist brushed against the cool, grey plastic, sensed rather than felt the hardness beneath. He took a deep breath and held it, passed his arm around her until the fingers of both hands latched. His head was inside the wardrobe but by holding his breath he avoided the intense smell of Mothaks.

He lifted her and turned, stepping one foot neatly behind the other and swung her into the room. The mirror fixed to the back of the right-hand door of the wardrobe briefly showed him a waltzing couple, the girl incongruously clad in crackling grey plastic, fastened with orange twine. He saw his face suspended over her shoulder and blew out his breath. Her weight rested against him, biting into his collarbone and shoulder. He pushed her away, blocking the mirror, steadied her with both hands. His room was small, oblong in shape, a difficult space in which to lay a large, unyielding object. He moved her to the right, lifting her like a dancer partnering the prima ballerina,

132

managed to hook his left foot under the wardrobe door, slamming it shut. The metal coat-hangers, pressed together, rattled loudly in the empty house. It was a choice of the bed, which he instinctively rejected, or the floor. He leaned her backwards, felt her feet slide on the carpet runner, lowered her to the floor. He straightened, red-faced from his exertions, panting. He flicked a lock of reddish-sandy hair from his forehead and looked at the displaced runner, rucked and bunched against the skirting board. Where it normally lay, the linoleum showed brighter and lighter on either side of her stiff, covered legs. He turned back to the wardrobe, carefully moved his clothes and the Mothaks along the rail, spacing them correctly and started to close the doors against the smell. On impulse, much as he had bought them, he reached in and snatched the white trousers from their hanger, setting it swinging and metallically clattering. He tossed the trousers onto the bed and stood, hands on his narrow hips, looking down at her, an encumbrance, a burden, a problem that had to be solved.

His parents were due at Luton airport at ten fifty tomorrow morning. He had promised to meet them in the red Golf his father had reluctantly lent him during their fortnight in Spain. Between then and now – a glance at his Timex showed it was five minutes to nine – she must be disposed of. He had no real plan, only a series of steps, fixed in an ordered sequence in his mind, towards the goal. He stepped over her and went out onto the landing, closing the door behind him. A grey, overcast dusk pressed at the skylight above him, at the inconveniently high window at the top of the stairs. He ran lightly down these and passed along the corridor beside the stairs into the kitchen. He paused just inside the door, his hand on the light-switch, waiting for the humming flickering strip-light to steady and flash on. The light hurt his eyes, making him close them for a moment. He did not open a window or the glass and wood back door even though the kitchen felt stale and warm. He did not draw the curtains, either. The harsh light turned the windows, the glass door to mirrors in which he observed his own swift, sure movements as he placed a piece of thick-sliced bread in the toaster, took the small, black, non-stick pan from the cupboard beneath the sink and, whistling, set about scrambling eggs.

It was an indulgence of his, when alone and able to prepare his own meals, to eat standing up at the draining board. He did not consider why he liked to do this, though would probably now have said that it cut down on the attendant chores. He did not need to set the blue Formica-topped table or swab it down afterwards, carefully catching the crumbs in his hand, carefully carrying them to the pedal bin beside the sink unit. He liked watching his reflection chew and swallow in the window. And there was another advantage. He could wash the non-stick pan and the wooden spoon while he ate, could dry them while finishing the last mouthful, his plate, knife and fork already soaking in the sink. While he waited for the electric kettle to boil, he washed and dried these objects, spooned Nescafé into a Thermos flask, rinsed and dried the spoon. When the water boiled, he carefully filled the flask, stoppered and capped it. To the right of the sink unit was a door, its silver-coloured key gleaming in the lock. Flask tucked under his arm, his arm and side surprised at its coolness since it contained such heat. This thought, or realisation made him cluck his tongue impatiently. He knew the principle of the Thermos flask as well as he knew the constituents of air or the action of yeast in bread making. Eighteen months' unemployment had not dulled or softened his brain and he must be vigilant not to let it. The door opened into a square utility room. Kerry Mather did not bother to put on the light, but crossed it, his elongated shadow preceding him, by the light from the kitchen. Another door opened into the garage where he switched on a single sixty-watt bulb slung in the exposed and dusty rafters. This direct access to the garage was, in his opinion, the only convenient thing about the house his father scrupulously maintained, according to an annual timetable, and which his mother dusted and scrubbed and cosseted according to a fixed weekly routine.

He had washed and waxed the Golf twice in his parents' absence, though not on the days ordained by his father. This slight variation in the car's routine had given him a guilty sense of pleasure. He had taken it that afternoon to the garage, had filled the tank and checked the oil, put air into two tyres. The manager, Mr Hobson, had asked if he was getting her ready to collect his parents and he had said yes, and yes, they were having a good time. He had received two postcards. As expected, he showed Mr Hobson the second one and the man had read with pleasure the closing lines. *Remember us to all who remember us.*

Now she stood, shining in the light, ready to go. Kerry Mather opened the nearside door and put the flask on the passenger seat on top of the folded map, which he had studied without agreeing or fixing a route and precise destination. He walked around the car, whistling softly, considering. She would not fit into the boot, so much was obvious at a glance. Not now when she was stiff and unpliable. It must be the back seat, therefore, or better yet, the floor behind the front seats. He contemplated the space carefully, then adjusted the passenger seat, sliding it forward a couple of inches. This reminded him that tomorrow, when he reached Luton airport, he must readjust the driving seat to accommodate his father's longer legs and bigger frame. He left the nearside back door open, both doors to the utility room. It was almost dark now. He put out the kitchen light but illuminated the passage and stairwell. At the foot of the stairs he paused and moved a small table and a blue and white jar of pampas grass out of harm's way. Both left small indentations in the sage green carpet which reassured him he could replace both exactly, so that his parents would never know that they had been moved.

As he ran up the stairs two at a time, feeling light and fit, he remembered the dead weight of her when he had carried her up, how he had thought he might not make it. Then she had been still warm and pliable, had fitted bent into the boot, had flopped heavily over his shoulder. Now, although she was stiff and more cumbersome, she felt lighter, or perhaps he had grown stronger, more confident in the time she had spent in the house. He dragged her feet first onto the landing then bent and lifted her upright again, his legs aching with the strain, grunting with the effort. He embraced her again and lifted her, eyes unfocused against the grey plastic and felt carefully for each tread with his feet. At the bottom, which he seemed to reach in a surprisingly short time, he rested, leaning her body against the banister, tossing his head to flick the hair out of his eyes. He puffed and panted, orchestrated his breath as he had seen gymnasts and weightlifters do on the television. But there was no time like the present, he thought, and leaving her propped, replaced the table, fitting each foot carefully into the indented marks, and then the vase, careful not to disturb the arranged fronds of pampas grass.

He considered trying to carry her horizontally, tucked under one arm, as it were, resting against his hip. He felt sure he could manage the weight once he found her centre of balance, but he foresaw difficulties with her stiff legs sticking out behind him, imagined them jammed, for instance, between kitchen door frame and stove. He rejected the idea and readied himself for the now familiar embrace, pulling her weight out from the banisters and taking it against his own braced body, folding his arms around her, lacing his fingers together. He began to whistle 'I could have danced all night' and lifted her, swung her easily towards the kitchen door and carried her straight through, gracefully negotiating the necessary twists and turns occasioned by the stove, the kitchen table, the larder cupboard. He put her down but did not release her in the utility room, went through his breathing routine, the expelled air briefly flattening the grey plastic against her face, giving her a momentary semblance of human features. He averted his face slightly and blew harmlessly over her shoulder, then lifted her again and, at a sort of awkward run, got her to the garage door.

She was heavy now, her weight dragging painfully at his shoulders. He held her, peered around her, considering how best to get her into the car. It was obvious that she must be placed in the horizontal plane, on her side. Then, with one lift, for which, in view of his tiring body he must prepare himself carefully, he could get at least half her body into the car. He lifted and turned her, his arm slipping on the plastic, failed to find her centre of balance and felt her swinging out of control. Her head cracked against the floor of the car, making it rock. He wished now that he had not eaten first. The scrambled eggs seemed locked in his chest and acid stung his mouth. Squatting, he laid her down. He waited, resting, considering the problem. Her head was just below the floor of the car, having slipped back after striking it. He must lift her again, push, slide her forward. He clambered over her, into the garage itself, certain that he could get a better purchase, leverage from this angle, by leaning into the utility room. He grasped her approximately around the waist, slid the weight of her onto his bent and sloping thighs, supported her thus for a moment, then heaved and slid. The car rocked, one spring squeaking slightly. The grey package of her legs stuck out straight, not dipping, showing that the worst of his task was over. He walked around the car, opened the offside door and, anxious now to be finished, tugged at her grimly, sliding her towards him. The thin plastic tore a little in his hands. He grasped a hard arm and pulled. She was in. He closed both doors carefully and switched off the garage light.

He was sweating, breathing unevenly. He saw that it was fully dark now. Through the kitchen windows and glass door, rectangles of light glowed in other houses backing onto theirs. An aeroplane throbbed overhead, its red and green and white lights clear against the dark sky. Kerry Mather stooped a little, his muscles tired, to glimpse the aircraft. Tomorrow morning his parents, Muriel and Donald Mather, would step from such a craft and he must be there to meet them, the car seats adjusted, his fixed smile at the ready. It was now ten fifteen.

As he went for the last time up the stairs, the muscles in the backs of his thighs aching pleasantly, he pulled off his short-sleeved cotton-knit shirt and, aware of his mother's disapproval, used it as a makeshift towel to dab under his arms, wipe the damp back of his neck. In his room, already curtained, he sat on the bed to unlace and remove his black training shoes, stood to unzip and lower his jeans. He took an aerosol from the shelf above his bed and sprayed under each arm, the scent of the

137

anti-perspirant clean and sharp on his nose. Then he pulled on the white cotton trousers, zipped and buttoned them. They were an act of defiance, which he consciously enjoyed. Not only were they impractical for the task ahead of him but white was a stupid colour to wear at night, on a mission of some secrecy. He knew all this and that was why he wanted to wear them, hoped that when he returned they would be stained and marked with grass and dirt. He could picture his mother's face as she fished them, appalled, from the Ali Baba basket in the bathroom.

'Kerry? What on earth have you been doing in these stupid trousers? I told you they were impractical. I can't think what possessed you to buy them. It's not as though you have money to throw away. How I'll get these stains out, I'll never know.'

Kerry Mather laughed out loud, feeling his taut ribcage sing beneath his fingers, resonate with his pleasure.

And perhaps his father, puzzled expression over horn-rimmed spectacles, would come to see what all the fuss was about. His mother waving the soiled trousers at her husband, his baleful look at Kerry.

'If you were earning, it would be a different story. Your mother's quite right. If you were earning, you'd soon learn. Do you know the price of a packet of biological washing powder? Not to mention the electricity, the water rates, the wear and tear on the Hoovermatic? The sooner you get a job, my boy, the better for all of us.'

He felt cold. It wasn't as though he hadn't tried. Over three hundred letters he'd written in the last eighteen months. His eyes went quickly to the bulging expanding file on his narrow desk. Each letter filed, proof of his efforts. In addition, the phone calls in response to advertisements in the local papers, the unrecorded journeys clutching slips of paper from the Job Centre. It wasn't as though he hadn't tried. Sometimes it seemed he was just *intended* to be a statistic, one buried in the three million unemployed.

He pulled open a drawer, searched through it, found the navy-blue sweatshirt and yanked it roughly over his head, kneeing the drawer shut. He took a comb to his hair, spreading and bending his knees a little to fit his image into the mirror he had outgrown. Satisfied, he pocketed the comb in case the exertion ahead of him might cause him to need to tidy his hair again. Then he looked around the room, checking it. He straightened the runner, aligning it precisely, the bedspread, slipped on his black moccasin shoes and picked up the soiled shirt. This he dropped into the Ali Baba basket in the bathroom before going to relieve himself, as he had been taught. Never leave the house without. You never knew when you might want to go and public lavatories were not easily come by. Besides, they were such unpleasant, unhygienic places. And wash your hands afterwards and, for goodness sake, leave the towel tidy. Kerry Mather straightened it on its pristine rail, matching edges, smoothing creases, and then went downstairs.

Keys, lights, make sure everywhere is locked. The downstairs light left on to deter burglars, make the house look inhabited. Close each door after you, kitchen, utility room, garage. He felt a pang of excitement, freedom as he saw the car, gleaming, waiting, ready to go. Before opening the garage doors, he switched off the light. Someone was bound to notice him leaving so late at night and report it, but there was no need to give them encouragement by advertising. His father kept the hinges oiled, the garage doors correctly hung. They opened silently and easily. Kerry Mather got into the car and started it, let out the handbrake and let it roll down the short incline of the drive until the rear end was well clear of the garage doors. Then he went back, closed and locked them.

He had done little driving at night, his father being reluctant to lend him the car and a man who considered driving essentially a daytime activity. But when he had been allowed to borrow it, mostly for fishing trips, which often necessitated an early start, before dawn, he had particularly enjoyed the sense of privacy and quiet he associated with night-time driving. Once he was clear of the town, that is, though even there the comparative lateness of the hour had reduced the traffic to the occasional cruising police car, a few through-going lorries, young couples, lovers he supposed, fending off the end of a romantic evening. He found himself adjacent to a police car at slow traffic lights in the centre of town. The capped officer in the passenger seat did not glance at him but seemed sunk in some morose thoughts of his own. The sight of the car, the officers, did not alarm him or seem in any way a portent. He did not even think, as he waited for the lights to change, of the body in the back of his car. Instead, he reminded himself to accelerate properly when the lights changed, to show that he could drive well and was obedient to the highway code. In fact, it was the police car that bolted at the first gleam of orange and it had already turned off the main road ahead of him by the time he had changed gears.

He did not connect the police with the girl wrapped in two overlapping plastic sacks in the back of the car because he felt no guilt about or responsibility for her. He still did not believe that he had killed her, despite the yellowing purple marks on her neck which, with the passing days, had taken on the surreality of abstract tattoos. The whole thing had been a bizarre and stupid accident. About that he was absolutely clear. It was an accident that he had gone to Passington that day. He had intended to fish a mere ten miles this side of the city, about which he had read, but when he got there, he had been unable to find the keeper, obtain a permit, and he was not courageous enough to ignore the forbidding signs. So he had driven into the city, bored, thinking to get a sandwich, a cup of coffee, and having done that thought he might as well try the rather inviting-looking river which swept along one edge of the city, making a sort of barrier between town and country. There were other fishermen already stationed on the bank, a couple of schoolboys. It was better than nothing, a nice day, a pleasant spot and, besides, he had nothing better to do.

He had had no success, a couple of tiny perch that were hardly worth unhooking. He changed his bait and propped his rod, settled down on the bank, half-dozing, half-watching the passers-by. He had noticed the youth particularly only because of his hair, shorn at the sides, worn in a sort of curled crest which fell in what Kerry Mather thought were called ringlets

140

between his shoulder blades. Even so he had been no more than a passer-by, briefly noticed, as quickly forgotten. It was the fact that he had turned suddenly into the coppice of trees which bounded the towpath some fifty yards further on that retained his interest. He wondered why the boy had turned so sharply and unexpectedly into the trees and came up with the obvious answer, prompted by his own bladder. His mother's dictum about the availability of public conveniences had seemed especially true. After leaving the coffee shop he had looked for one and failed to find any. Collecting the car from the car park and driving down to the water's edge his need – more precautionary than pressing, then – had slipped his mind. The youth's sudden, surprising quitting of the path had reminded him of it and awoken him to the fact that it was now urgent. He had waited, uncomfortable, continually watching for the boy to re-emerge, resume his way. He did not want to follow him, to advertise the fact that he had deduced the boy's purpose, had a similar need of his own, but when the youth did not reappear, and his need became greater, he had decided that perhaps he had been mistaken, that the coppice was a short-cut to somewhere or that there was a path he could not see that led to some habitation or place of work, a boatyard, possibly.

He glanced to left and right. There was no one about but another absorbed fisherman snoozing in the shade of a golf umbrella. Kerry Mather checked his line, the fastness of his rod and, with some agitation, hurried along the path to the edge of the coppice, entering at a point considerably closer to his fishing station than had the boy. But the trees there had been too sparsely spaced. Even if he had stood directly behind one, facing the path, his stance would have declared his purpose to anyone passing along the footpath. Ahead he could glimpse a field of long and waving grass. Only to his left did the trees promise a concealing privacy. And there was no turning back then, even though he half-feared coming face to face with the boy, because his bladder adamantly forbade it. He had gone on, his mind focused only on his need, his vision narrowed to find a spot, any spot, sufficiently screened from path and field, where he could, as quickly as possible, relieve himself. He found it with gratitude and set about his essential purpose.

He had almost finished when he saw them, or heard them rather, his heart skipping, his fingers hurrying to cover himself. Instinctively he sought for the source of the noise which had alerted him to some other presence and there, at a distance of some yards, against a tree, he had seen them. At first he thought they were simply necking, was as anxious not to disturb them as he was to adjust his clothing and get away. But slowly, as he looked, not out of interest or prurience but to be alert for any sign that they saw him, he read the message of displaced clothing, of movements and saw that they were making love.

He blushed now as then, glad this time of the dark, of being out of the town, on an unlit B road, flanked by fields and hedges. He had stayed, frozen to the spot, watching them without meaning to. That, too, had been an accident. It was all accident. He had been too scared and embarrassed to move, afraid of attracting their attention, for what could they make of his presence, how construe it but in the worst possible way? It was only when they unglued their bodies, stood for a moment intimately exposed that his head had been able to rule his legs. He had moved backward, cautiously, trusting that in their post-coital preoccupation they would not notice a rustle or the snapping of a twig beneath his foot. He had turned and hurried, glad now of the sparseness of the trees, regained the path as quickly as possible. He only wanted one thing at that moment: to get away. He felt obscurely agitated, his mind jumping at what he had seen and should not have seen.

Even when he reached the car, he still felt uneasy. He had opened the boot, preparing to pack his rod and bait tins, but was shaking so much, felt so odd in himself, that he had decided to drink some coffee from the Thermos flask he had been saving for the homeward journey. He had sat on the edge of the open hatchback, holding the plastic mug in both hands, blowing on the too-hot liquid, when the youth had passed by again, walking quickly, nonchalantly, his hands thrust into the jeans' pockets. Kerry Mather had turned his face away,

142

unable to look at him, afraid to look at him.

The youth's pace, stance, look, all seemed so ordinary, so casual that Kerry Mather wondered if he had really seen what he had seen, which disturbed him and blighted his day. It was not until the boy had disappeared from view around a bend in the river, towards the bridge that spanned it at the city's edge, that he thought again of the girl. They had met, made love and should, by all the laws of reason, have strolled back together, arms about each other, talking softly. He became alarmed for the girl, told himself not to be so stupid, that she had left by another route, that it had been a lunchtime tryst and each had had to hurry away to work or some other demand upon their time. But to where could you hurry through a field of waist-high grass? He had seen no other obvious exit except, of course, the towpath and on that she had not set foot. He dithered for several minutes, trying to convince himself that she had emerged unnoticed, walked off in the opposite direction. In any case it was none of his business. Yet he had to know what had happened to the girl. He realised now, with a feeling of panic, that he had wanted to see her as he had seen the boy, her lover, *afterwards*.

And he had seen her, seated, dishevelled, her back propped against the very same tree that had served them as an upright bed, weeping, weeping in such a terrible, desperate way as to touch if not break his heart. He had dropped to one knee beside her, had reached to comfort her and she had beat at him with her small fists, yelling obscenities, swearing at him. Too late, Kerry Mather had realised that she had mistaken his intentions, thought that he wanted what she had so willingly given her lover. The thought sickened him. As if he would go where that other boy had been. He knew about disease, personal hygiene. He had become angry in his turn, as angry at her presumption as she was at his simple, well-meant attempts to console her. In addition there had been the need to make her quiet, be still, to understand.

She had been very still then, her head lolling to one side. Kerry Mather had felt pins and needles in his right calf, the knee still pressing into the hard, dry earth. He had touched her silky hair, turned her limp face towards him. She wore a funny, glazed expression and could not hold her head up to look at him. When he released it, it flopped down and to one side, her hair falling across her face, obscuring it.

He was perspiring now, could feel it soaking into his sweatshirt where his back pressed against the driving seat. He had to stop, rest awhile. His hands were trembling on the wheel. He concentrated on the road ahead, searching for a lay-by or somewhere he could pull safely over. He slowed so as to miss no opportunity and because he knew he was not driving well. A field gate was caught in his headlights, the verge widening before it sufficiently to provide a temporary, improvised parking space. He drew up and switched off the engine, killed all but his sidelights. He let out his breath in a kind of shiver and rubbed his upper arms for warmth and comfort.

Only when he was back at the car, his mind hazy, the fishing tackle loaded, did he realise the girl was dead. The one thing he felt certain about, apart from the fact that it had been a meaningless accident, was that he could not leave her there, alone and dead in the coppice of trees. Even now when she had become a burden to him, he did not renege on that feeling of certainty.

There had been no one about. The riverbank had that deserted, sleepy quality that he always associated with hot, tedious summer afternoons. It was as though the world slept or had gone into spasm, awaiting the cooler breeze of evening. It was a quality of light he had recognised in certain Impressionist paintings, the most famous ones, which induced the same feelings of impotent lethargy in him, as though the magic of siesta, of frozen time, had somehow passed him by.

He had not paused to think about it then. It was evident that the towpath was deserted, silent. He had backed the car along to the coppice, carried her, heavy and floppy, from the trees and folded her, without ceremony or much care, into the boot and driven home. It had been impossible to leave her there.

He opened the offside door a little, blocking it with his foot, so that the roof light went on. He pulled the map from beneath the Thermos flask and spread it across the steering wheel. In this way, if another car should pass, he would not look odd or remarkable. Besides, he realised, his sketchy plan had run out. He had to decide now where to take her. He bent over the map, forcing his eyes to focus on the maze of lines and pale contours, the tiny lettering in the dim light.

He knew now, of course, that she was sixteen and was named Lenora Mitchell. So much he had discovered from the national newspaper that was delivered each weekday to his parents' home, and which, in their absence, he was able to read first and at his leisure. Passington had been the clue that had enabled him to make the connection, that and the date which he had checked against his father's calendar. He had set himself, deliberately, to watch the television and had been bored by some studio discussion between an angry policeman and an angry interviewer about some man who had been questioned and released, a man whose sketched, black and white face had been flashed on the screen and who, in Kerry Mather's considered opinion, looked like a murderer as he, most definitely, did not. There had been a picture of her, too, on that or another occasion, interspersed with shots of lines of men walking through the silky field, searching. His memory was hazy as to the sequence of events, the passage of time, as though that blank period between her hitting out at him and her subsequent complete stillness, was not yet lived through but could reach out to him and suck him back into its strange timelessness at will. But sight of her picture, whenever it was, had prompted him to open the right side of his wardrobe and take her out, sheathe her in two overlapping plastic sacks, bind them with orange twine. After that he had been able to think about the presence of a body in the house in a clear and logical way. His eyes, thereafter, skated over newspaper reports mentioning her and he stopped watching the television news. She was Lenora Mitchell, she was dead and in the back of his father's, Donald Mather's car, but the only thing that mattered was that he had, now, to leave her somewhere, get rid of her before his parents returned at ten fifty tomorrow morning. This morning, he corrected himself, looking at the faint dial of his watch. He addressed himself to the map, tracing lines. No cars passed. No midnight stroller appeared out of the dark. He poured himself a little coffee and drank it, blowing on it to cool it, shook the empty mug onto the grass beside the car, replaced it on the Thermos. Then he drove off again, calm and alert.

It was at a crossroads, an archetypal meeting of four ways, marked with a typical four-fingered signpost that he next stopped and read: Lunton, Colby; Brindsleigh, Oversleigh; Brindsleigh Dam; Bowleigh Highers, Anderton. He consulted the map again. The left-hand fork was soon and clearly marked as an unmade road ending abruptly and pointlessly in a field. He folded the map and turned left. The car swayed when the metalled surface gave out. The 'road' was two deep ruts, strongly tyre-marked, suggesting heavy farm or construction vehicles, their tracks baked hard by the recent hot, dry weather. With only his sidelights on, Kerry Mather fitted the car's wheels into these ruts confident that he would leave no tell-tale marks of his own, and proceeded at a slow five miles an hour. The track rose slightly, steadily and he saw a cube-shaped building, a sort of concrete hut, loom against the night sky. He stopped and got out to explore. Beyond the building, which was windowless and had a metal door set flush, the ground sloped quite steeply downward. There was the sound of running water. A stream, low from the lack of rain, trickled and tinkled away into trees. Adjacent to it, set into the slope was a concrete pit, the yawning mouth of an underground pipe, a cantilevered, grey metal gate. All this he saw in a glance or two, by the beam of a flashlight, sparingly used. There was a little water in the bottom of the concrete pit, a dead rat floating on its surface, a dented Coke can. He saw how, when the stream was swollen, the cantilevered gate would direct some of the water into the pit and so prevent flooding. The underground pipeline, now just a black hole in the grey concrete, would carry the water away, elsewhere.

He climbed the slope, slightly out of breath and put the flashlight back into the glove compartment of the car, where his father always kept it, for emergencies. When he straightened up, the moon appeared, a pale slice between clouds. It made his white trousers shine very white, without a mark on them as far as he could tell. He closed the front door and opened the back, inserted both hands under the stiff weight of her and pulled. She slid out easily, lay on the hard earth at his feet. He saw that the plastic bags had come adrift, no longer overlapped but wrinkled up and down her body. It did not matter now, he thought and bent, tugged at the knot of orange twine until it came loose and her makeshift girdle slipped from her. He wound the twine neatly around his fingers, tucked in its loose end and pocketed it. He crouched beside her, pushed. Reluctantly, she turned over. In this way, steadily, taking his time, pausing to rectify his breathing between each effort, he rolled her to the top of the incline and then, with his foot, gave her one last push, saw her grey, rustling shape roll away down the steeper slope, propelled by her own weight and momentum.

There was no splash of water. The moon was obscured by a cloud. He hesitated, thinking he had done enough, thinking that perhaps he should go back and fetch the flashlight. For a moment he was frightened, felt the sweat break out on his body again. He fancied he heard approaching cars, voices in the sound of the water. He made himself go back down the slope, unlit, slipped and lost his footing, put out a hand to steady himself. He fell onto his backside and slid forward. His white trousers, he thought, would be filthy. He wanted to laugh at that, but stopped himself. Slowly he got onto all fours, head facing down the slope and moved towards her, deliberately scuffing his knees on the ground. He reached her, touched plastic, the linen of her skirt, and, by stretching over her discovered why she had not fallen into the concrete pit. A ledge, some six inches in height, was raised above the level of the earth. He straightened up, kneeling. It was a simple matter to lift her one last time, roll her onto the ledge and let her fall. He heard her hit the water with a splash as loud as a gunshot. It almost hurt his ears. He waited, listening, listening to the sound of air bubbles rising and settling, listening until there was only the sound of running water. Then he stood up and faced the slope, climbed it thankfully, wiping his hands on his white trousers. He began to whistle softly as he reached the waiting car. He climbed in, took off the handbrake and rolled silently back towards the road.

Thirty-six hours at Passington police station had transformed Michael Stones and given Riley a grudging respect for him. A brownish stubble had taken the powder from his face and confirmed what Riley had first suspected: that his hair was dyed. His curls and ringlets were sadly in need of attention.

'You look a mess,' Riley said, twisting a ruler in his fingers, leaning back from his desk.

'Yeah?' He seemed hunched in the grey tracksuit that they had allowed him to wear over his white shorts and T-shirt, as though he was perpetually cold.

'Definitely,' Riley confirmed. 'But your story checks out.'

'I told you.'

Riley swung into the desk, looked at the reports and statements. Either all of Michael's mates and half his family were in on it, or the boy was in the clear. Every movement checked. His alibi, all but the time he had spent alone with Leni Mitchell, had been substantiated and verified.

'You could have thrown her in the river, of course,' Riley said conversationally. 'Before you went back to college, I mean.'

'Yeah? Then why haven't you found her body?'

'Oh she could be anywhere, out to sea by now.'

'Well, if she is, I didn't put her there.'

'No. You just left her, walked away from her. You'd got what you wanted and you didn't give a toss.'

'If you say so.' Michael had learned quickly not to rise to Riley's needling bait and Riley respected him for that, that and his consistency. In all the questionings and re-questionings, he had never wavered from his initial tale, added only one particular.

'That red car bothers me,' Riley said. 'You're absolutely sure it was there when you went back to college?'

'Positive.'

'But you didn't see anyone with it? No driver? No one sitting in the back, the passenger seat? Is that right?'

'I didn't notice. That's all I can say. There might've been, there might not. I just didn't notice.'

'Pity.'

'Yeah.'

Consistency of that sort, accuracy in every checkable particular was, as the old man said, either the work of a master criminal, the fruit of months, at least, of planning and conspiracy, or the simple, honest truth. And if everything checkable was true, then why not Michael Stones's account of his meeting with Leni? Even there he had not attempted to present himself in a good light. He had probably told the truth.

'It's frustrating,' Riley said aloud.

'What?'

'The possibility that you've told me the truth.'

'I thought that was what you wanted.'

'Of course. But it's still bloody frustrating.'

'Sorry.'

'Now you're lying.'

'Right.'

They looked at each other. The boy's tired, dull eyes moved away first.

'You know, if you got yourself a decent haircut and a bit of moral responsibility, you wouldn't be a bad lad.'

'Stuff it,' Michael said. 'You don't have any right to lecture me.'

'A friendly word of advice . . . ' Riley said and spread his arms to appeal his innocence.

'Thanks.'

'That's better.'

Just one more time, Riley thought. Just one more angle. If he could only find the trigger that would throw Stones, crack him open. The internal telephone on his desk buzzed. Michael Stones seemed to sink smaller in his chair. Apparently he neither welcomed nor resented the interruption. Riley let it ring again, watching him.

'Riley,' he said into the receiver.

'Have you released Mr Stones yet, Riley?'

'No, sir. Just about to . . . '

'Get on with it, man. There have been developments.'

'Oh? What, sir?'

'A body. Get rid of Stones and come up and see me. Now.'

Riley was given no time to reply. He looked at the receiver, then replaced it.

'If she was to turn up, I mean dead, where do you reckon that would be?'

Slowly Michael turned his head to look at him. His expression clearly asked if Riley was serious. He saw that he was, in a way.

'Timbuctoo?' He shrugged.

Riley took a long breath, let it out slowly, a kind of sigh.

'I'll remember that, if she does. Now clear out.'

Tom read the letter in silence, at the table in the window, wearing his white towelling robe. Karen, who had hurried into her clothes while he went to collect the mail, thinking, for some reason that she did not understand, that she had better be ready for anything, tried not to watch him as she waited for the kettle to boil.

'Shit.' He held the letter out towards her, his head turned away, massaging his forehead with his right hand. She took it eagerly, saw the black crest and the heading, Breeton College. He had not got it. She wanted to cry out with relief. The light in the room seemed to become suddenly much brighter. But she could only stare at him, realised that he might even be crying.

'I'm sorry. Honest I am.' She went to him and touched his shoulder, afraid that he would shrug her off. She felt the muscles bunched and tense and began to massage them. She put the letter on the table beside him. 'At least you didn't lose out to anyone,' she said, trying to be cheerful. 'They say they're not making an appointment.'

150

'And, significantly, they don't invite me to reapply when they advertise again,' he said angrily, standing up, brushing her aside. 'That is the form, you know.'

He stood in the bay window, looking out, his arms wrapped around himself, his back rejecting her. The kettle boiled, clicked off. She looked at it, then back at him, not knowing what to do.

'Is it?' she said. 'I don't know about these things. I'll make some coffee.' He said nothing. She made herself concentrate on the jar of Maxwell House, the mugs. She carried his to him and said, 'Drink this.'

'In a minute. Put it down.'

'Don't shut me out. Let me help.' She had promised herself she could handle anything, except his getting the job. Now she could not feel that same certainty, was afraid of his mood, to touch him.

'You never wanted me to get it anyway,' he complained.

'I was afraid of losing you.'

'Rubbish.'

'You'd have gone away, had to. I didn't see how I'd fit in. I was just being selfish.'

'Oh Christ.' He turned and grabbed her clumsily, pulling her against him, burying his face in her hair. She let him crush her, gently stroked his back. Let him cry, she thought. Go on, have a good cry. I can handle anything. 'I'm sorry, so sorry.'

'Don't be silly.'

'I'm just scared. I don't know how we'll manage.'

'You said "we".'

'Well, I'm not going anywhere, am I?'

'There'll be other jobs, if you really want one.'

'You,' he said, hugging her more loosely now, 'you're too damned good for me.'

'Yeah, I know,' she said. 'Drink your coffee.'

He swallowed, hid his face, rubbing his sleeve across it, made a business of picking up the mug, keeping his face from her.

'At least it's a nice day,' he said. 'Small mercies and all that.'

'Don't. It's all right. You have a right to be disappointed.'

151

'All rejections hurt. Yeah, yeah. I know.'

'You can paint,' she said quickly. 'There's still five weeks of the holiday left. You could do a lot of work.'

'Yes.'

'Now this is out of the way, you could concentrate.'

'Maybe you're right.'

'You know I am. And you could get in touch with your old gallery, let them know you're working. And then there's the Passington autumn exhibition. You ought to enter a couple of canvases for that. It would be a start, love. Please.'

'Are you organising me?'

'Yes. Well, somebody's got to.'

He smiled at her.

'I think,' he said, 'I'll go and have a bath. OK?'

'Fine.'

'I'll take this with me,' he said gesturing with the mug. 'I'll think about it. Really think about it. Promise.' He kissed her cheek.

She wanted to sing and dance and skip about the room, to throw up the window and yell, He's mine. It's all right. I'm happy. But she knew she could only rejoice privately, inwardly. She was ashamed even of thinking that she possessed him. One day she would have to let him go. She knew that with her old, familiar certainty, but it did not chill her. Not today. She would make things work for him and take her chance. That's all anyone can ask, really, she thought. She shook out the duvet, tidied the bed. Over the back of the easy chair on which Tom's clothes were strewn, hung the blue costume she was making for Robert Luman. The loose, pyjama-like trousers still needed hemming. It wouldn't take her long. Just a few final adjustments. She began to hum as she carried the clothes and her small work-basket to the light and sat to thread her needle. Her sewing machine, on which she had done the bulk of the work, was in her own room near the tech. She realised, with a start of excitement, that now Tom knew about the job, they could think seriously about living together. Perhaps not until his divorce was through. They would have to be discreet, of course. The tech was bound to have objections, even though most people knew they were having an affair . . . It was a possibility. In fact, today, her life was suddenly full of possibilities.

Tom came back into the room, wrapped damply in the robe, and began pulling out drawers, searching for clothes.

'Let's go out somewhere today,' he said. 'The sun's shining. Let's make a day of it. Karen?'

'Oh . . . '

'What?' He paused, frowning at her, his mood threatening to change.

'It's just . . . I've got to finish this. I promised. But it won't take long. Yes, let's—'

'No, forget it.' He slammed a door shut.

'Look, I promised—'

'I know.'

'That was a terrible thing I did. Mrs Luman's always been good to me. I'm fond of Robert. I caused them a lot of aggro—'

'And it was all my fault. Yes. I know.'

'I just want to say I'm sorry.'

'Fine.'

He began to dress, pulling his clothes on as though they had to be subdued. Karen stitched. How quickly possibilities get trampled underfoot. One stray word, she thought, an inflection ill considered.

'You could come with me,' she said, not very hopefully.

'Where?'

'Just while I drop this off. I won't be a minute. Then we can drive somewhere. You could make some sketches . . . '

'If you think I'm—'

'It'll take me half an hour to finish. I'll just drop it off and we can go anywhere you like.'

'No. You . . . get on with it.'

'Tom, please. It's important to me. It's like the job was to you, if you like. You can put that behind you now. I want to do the same with this. It won't take me long, love, honest.'

He looked at her. She thought she was going to cry. She'd spoiled everything. She only wanted to make it up to Mrs

Luman, Robert. She still felt that she had come close to destroying them, somehow. She sniffed, told herself she was being melodramatic. Tom's shadow fell on her. She did not dare to look up.

'You look good, sewing. You sew well, don't you?'

'I'm a bit slapdash. My sewing teacher'd have a fit if she saw these seams. "Unpick and do it again, Karen. *Properly*, this time."'

'Actually, what it is,' he said, reaching under her hair to fondle the nape of her neck, 'is I'm jealous.'

'What are you talking about?'

'I want a Superman outfit. Can't you just see me?' He stepped back, struck a pose, arms bent, flexing his muscles. Karen laughed.

'You're a nutter,' she said.

'Takes one to know one.'

'It's all right, then? You'll come? Over to Brindsleigh with me, and then we'll take off somewhere?'

'I'll go and fill the car up.'

'Oh, Tom . . .'

'And you can start designing me my own jumpsuit. Black, I think, don't you? And very figure-hugging.'

'You'll need a codpiece, then,' she grinned and ducked as he mock-swiped at her. The day was bright again. She made small, neat stitches, for Robert, Mrs Luman, for Tom. For making her happy.

Two farmworkers had found her while manoeuvring the spraying machine up past the dam to the field known as Brindsleigh Top which effectively marked the western limit of the parish. One of the plastic sacks had inflated, buoying her. Below it, her hands were visible, part of her white blouse and navy-blue skirt. One of the men had gone to fetch Constable Smith while the other, rather nervously, stayed with her, pacing up and down. Jolley was supervising the recovery of the body; then it would be brought straight to Passington Police Headquarters Mortuary for autopsy and,

154

more importantly at this stage, for identification.

Riley pored over the map spread on Superintendent Tait's forbiddingly tidy desk, pinpointing the exact spot with a grubby forefinger. Bending his thumb he measured, approximately, the distance between the dam and Luman's bungalow. A mile and a quarter, he calculated, probably less. Call it a mile. It was too much of a coincidence.

'I know what you're thinking,' Tait said, hands in his pockets, rocking a little on the balls of his feet as he watched dark summer storm clouds massing over the cathedral. The weather was going to break. 'But get a positive identification first. She could be anybody.'

'I'll lay you any odds you like . . . '

'Fortunately, among my many vices, Riley, I do not number gambling.'

'No, sir. But you can't call this coincidence, sir.'

'I can't call it anything until I know who the poor unfortunate creature is. And even then . . . ' He came to the desk, waved his hands impatiently, signalling that Riley should remove the map. He did so, struggling with the folds.

'I reckon it's about a mile from Luman's house to this dam—'

'He can't drive. How would he have transported her? Is he strong enough to carry her, do you think, and unnoticed through the very heart of the village? Where has he concealed her all this time? It seems certain, by the way, that she has not been in the water more than a matter of hours. You're endowing a brain-damaged cabbage with the cunning and guile of a—'

'Murderer,' Riley said. 'Tracy Vorlander, Stella Lambert *saw* him . . . ' He did not want to think about Luman's supposed strength, about Luman in any physical sense at all. 'He brought her back there, somehow. On the train or . . . '

'You forget. He got a lift from Oversleigh, alone, from a reliable witness, a member of the British Legion and a parochial parish councillor . . . '

'Then he'd already done it. For Christ's sake, he couldn't take her home—'

155

'That's enough, Riley. I forbid you to say another word.'

The old man was rattled, worried. Riley could tell. He ran his hand across his sleek white head, the hair lacquered there, accentuating the outline of his skull. Broken veins were visible on his flushed cheekbones. Superintendent Tait was beginning to face the possibility – even Riley would not dare to put it higher than that, yet – that he had bungled it, that Riley had been right all along. It stood to reason. What other explanation could there possibly be? What other suspect had they ever had?

As though he could read Riley's thoughts, Tait said: 'It seems to me much more likely that the girl, in her distress, went off somewhere, hitch-hiking, possibly even in that red car young Mr Stones remembers. Is there anything on that yet, by the way?'

'A red car? No number, not even a make? Nothing, sir, no.'

'Well, keep on to it. Now you had better . . . ' He seemed to have an obstruction in his throat, cleared it, excused himself. 'You'd better organise the family to come and have a look at her. It may take a while to . . . er . . . get her out. There's no metalled road, I understand. We'll be informed, of course, as soon as she's on her way. And I don't want any leaks. I don't want anyone to know about this until the Mitchells have told us yea or nay.'

'Very good, sir,' Riley said, not trying very hard to suppress his grin. 'I'll see to it.' He moved towards the door.

'Er . . . Riley . . . ' Riley turned to him, eyebrows raised. 'There is something else . . . something I haven't had time to . . . uh . . . pass on to you. It's a matter of little importance . . . '

The wily old bastard had been concealing something. Riley knew it. Withholding information. He wondered what the book said about that, a superior officer withholding information . . .

'Our Mr Luman. He . . . er . . . in so far as he can be said to be capable of such an act . . . he made a sort of confession the other day, after that unfortunate leak of his picture. There's nothing to it, of course . . . '

'A confession . . . ?'

'Well, no, I . . . chose quite the wrong word. He turned up at the Brindsleigh police house, with a copy of the *Post*, saying something like . . . "I did it" . . . Words to that effect . . . '

'And you did nothing?'

'I'm still considering Constable . . . er . . . Smith's report. Mr Jolley is inclined—'

'Bugger Jolley,' Riley shouted and banged his fist onto the desk. 'I should have been told. He should have been arrested and brought here.'

'I disagree. And I shall overlook your . . . unpleasant remark about Mr Jolley. Anyway, you know now—'

'Indeed I do,' Riley said, realising that he need say nothing more, that anything he did say would only distract Tait from his true and deserved pain: the knowledge that he was, almost certainly, wrong and treading a very thin line. Riley, drawing himself up, experienced a throb of pleasure. He need do nothing, except relish Tait's first taste of panic, perhaps real fear. 'Thank you very much for telling me, sir,' he said. 'I appreciate it.'

'Not at all, Riley. Now off you go. And we'll keep each other closely informed.'

'Of course, sir.' Tait could not even look him in the eye. It was magic, pure magic. Riley, as he left the Superintendent's office, knew the meaning of the phrase, 'walking on air'.

The weather was going to break at last. Phyllis Luman went outside, to fetch the axe Peter Carter had been using yesterday to split logs for her 'against the winter', as he put it. She stood, holding the heavy axe in both hands, looking towards the church where the sky was most dark and livid. It would never do to leave the axe out in the rain, to rust . . . She supposed they meant well. They all agreed . . . And what were friends for but to heed when they gave advice? It was just that she had never left Robert before, had vowed that she never would the day that she accepted responsibility for him. They did not seem to understand this. And Robert had been very good, docile, withdrawn since Paula Brownlow had herded him back like a stray calf from the police house. Whatever had possessed him? What had gone on in his poor mind to make him . . . ? The axe suddenly felt very heavy and she lowered its metal head to the path and leaned her weight a little against the long handle. It was questions like these, endlessly going round and round in her head, that exhausted her and frayed her nerves. There was no answering them, anyway. There was a sensation, not unlike pins and needles in her left arm, a general lassitude that told her she was getting old, tired. She wasn't coping. They wanted her to go away, have a rest. A change, they said, was as good as a rest any day.

Dr Bugler started it when she came to look at Robert after the business at the police house.

'It's you I'm worried about,' she had said in that funny, mannish way of hers. 'You need a break. We ought to think about getting young Robert into a nice home for a couple of weeks, so that you could get away, have a proper rest.'

Phyllis would not hear of that. She would not have him in institutions, not even for a short stay, not while she had her health and strength. There would be plenty of time for that, too much in fact, when she was dead and buried. Dr Bugler had said no more then, but she must have said plenty elsewhere, for Pansy June was on the line before you could say 'knife', urging her to go to Suffolk with her. Phyllis had refused, of course, without thinking about it, for Robert was in no fit state to travel. The slightest disturbance now . . . But when she *did* think about it, the idea of seeing the old places again appealed to her with a sentimental tug. She had been nineteen when she left Suffolk and in the intervening years had been back only twice and not at all since the accident. Pansy had an aunt there – they had often talked of her – who had died recently. Pansy was planning to drive down that evening, after she had got the family settled, and spend the night and the following day sorting out her aunt's effects.

'Just a sort of general recce, you understand. I'll have to go down and dispose of them later but, gosh, I haven't a clue what she's got there. And apart from anything else, dear, I'd love

158

some company. I mean, I'm the last person to believe in spooks and things and Auntie Em was the most unspooky person ever, but you know how it is. It just isn't nice, somehow, being alone in an empty house. Of course, I know the house, but, well, it's not home, is it? So you see it really would be absolutely super for me and I *know* it would do you good. I only wish it could be longer but I've absolutely got to be back for the old people's tea . . . I know you understand. But even a short break, a change of air . . . Oh, do say yes, Phyll. I know you won't regret it.'

But they had not worn her down, even though Meg and Paula had followed hard on the heels of the telephone call, co-opted by Pansy and Dr Bugler, full of practical plans and reassurances that they would take care of everything. She had felt, suddenly, too tired to argue, resist. She had simply said, flatly, 'No.'

She would be able to rest now for she felt certain that Robert would remain calm. Too late, she recognised a pattern in his recent behaviour. So it had been in the early days, periods of hyperactivity, enthusiasms, culminating in acts of foolishness or temper caused by frustration, followed by a period of withdrawal, lethargy, silence. He had burned himself out. That was how the doctor had put it.

'Think of it like a short-circuit, Mrs Luman. We know that Robert's wiring isn't too good and sometimes, when he's very busy and trying to do things, it gets overloaded and eventually, bang! It shorts out. Then he needs to rest, to give the old wiring time to get back in working order. Semi-working order, I should say.'

It had been so long since he had experienced one of these cycles that Phyllis had ceased to be vigilant, to read the signs. Not that there was much one could do, except ride it out, be watchful. She had realised that the circuit had shorted, the cycle ended after Paula Brownlow brought him back, when he had clung to her like a baby, sucking his thumb, his eyes distantly troubled. He had slept like one unconscious, curled small like the foetus he had once been. She was certain that it had begun, this cycle, the day he had gone to Passington, and, of course, all that business with the police had only exacerbated it. She had

159

blamed herself for getting it wrong but she blamed them more
. . . Thank God nothing worse had happened than that young
Mrs Smith had had a bit of a scare. Poor Robert.

Phyllis Luman shook her head and tried to lift the weight of
the axe. It seemed too heavy for her. Why, only last year she
had chopped her own logs. She put both hands on the haft of it,
heard herself grunt like an animal as she managed to raise it.
Breathless, her head swimming a little, she carried the axe
indoors and placed it in the hall cupboard.

She was done in. There was a sort of relief in admitting it as
she leaned her shoulder and head against the cupboard door.
She felt herself begin to slide. It was so silly, almost comical.
The sound that reached her ears as she slid slowly to the floor
was not laughter, though she wanted to laugh. The knuckles of
her right hand struck something hard and hurt. She thought, I
must have flung out my hand to save myself. And yet there was
nothing to save herself from.

She fell quite gently, was just having a little lie-down . . . On
the floor? In the hall? She tried to laugh again. Now Meg would
really think she'd been at the sherry bottle. The sound in her
ears was strange, a sort of laboured, breathless breathing. Just a
little rest, she thought, for a minute or two and then . . . She
slipped away gratefully, into a swirling darkness.

'Five minutes. I promise. Not a second more.' Karen Ashburton
jumped out of the car, snatched up the plastic bag in which she
had folded the costume, and ran quickly up the path. Finishing
it and ironing it had taken longer than she had promised and to
placate Tom she had suggested a pub lunch *en route* so there
wasn't much of the day left. She did not like the look of the sky,
either. She rang the bell, shuffled her feet anxiously, willing
Mrs Luman to hurry. She glanced back at the car, saw with relief
that Tom was unfolding *The Guardian*, spreading it across the
steering wheel to read. She pressed the bell again, heard its
slightly asthmatic buzz, stepped back a little staring hard at the
door, waiting for the familiar, refracted figure to appear behind
the stippled glass. No one came. Surely they could not be out,

160

not at a time like this, at this time of day? Karen stepped smartly between the rose-bushes and looked into the un-curtained sitting-room window. The room looked untidy, as it had on her last visit, but quite obviously lived-in, occupied. The door into the hall stood open and through it, putting her hand up to shield her eyes from the light, she saw a hand lying, half-clenched, on the floor, the cuff of Phyllis Luman's pale grey cardigan.

'Oh my God . . . '

Her skirt snagged on a rose-bush as she hurried back to the door but she did not feel it. Bending, she could just make out a huddled shape on the floor. It was like looking under water. The shape had an indefinite, shifting outline. Colours swam, the grey of her cardigan, the blue of her skirt, splashes of brighter pink that Karen thought must be her apron.

Tom looked up, surprised, a ready smile spreading as she dashed back to the car.

'That really was—'

'Tom, something's happened. Come and help me, quick.'

She did not wait for him to reply, feared that he would protest. She bent on hands and knees to the low slit of the letterbox, yelled through it.

'Mrs Luman? Robert? Mrs Luman?' Reaching up in panic for the bell-push again, her hand struck against Tom.

'What is it?'

'She's lying there . . . Look . . . ' He stooped over her shoulder, his eyes close to the frosted glass. 'She might be dead,' Karen said, able to admit her worst fear now. 'Robert . . . ' She scrambled up, made towards Robert's window. Tom grabbed her arm, held her back.

'What?'

'Calm down. If she hasn't put the safety catch on . . . ' Karen stared helpless, uncomprehending, as he pulled out his scuffed and battered wallet, flipped it open and pulled out his cheque card. It was a simple Yale lock. The door did not fit completely flush. Mesmerised, Karen drew closer to him, watched him slip the card into the crack between door and frame, his lips pressed

161

together in concentration. She held her breath, saw the card strike an unseen obstacle, slowly, slowly move again.

'Oh . . . ' she gasped as the door swung open. She pushed it wider, ran in. Tom followed her, his shadow falling comfortingly over her as she knelt beside the crumpled woman.

'Don't move her . . . '

'No.' She felt gently for a pulse in the neck. 'She's warm . . . '

'She's breathing,' Tom said sharply. 'You can hear it.' Turning, he saw the phone and crossed to it with one stride. Karen smoothed the soft white hair from Phyllis's colourless face.

'Ambulance. It's an emergency,' she heard him say and there was strength and calm in his voice. If she had ever doubted that she loved him . . .

'It'll be all right,' she told the still woman. 'An ambulance is coming.' Tom stepped over the prone body, went into the bedroom and returned carrying the soft, pink quilt. Karen helped him spread it over her, tuck it around her.

'That'll keep her warm. Is there anyone we should phone?'

Karen stared at him, wide-eyed. Robert. Where was Robert? She got up, turned to his door.

'Where are you going?'

'Robert,' she whispered and slowly, quietly opened the door. Peering over the shelves that boxed in his bed, she saw him, lying on his back, the covers pulled up to his shoulders, the sadly familiar blue hat glowing against the pillows. The relief was enormous, freed her frozen brain. She pulled the door to.

'I'd better stay with him. If he sees . . . Call Paula Brownlow and Meg Sowers. They'll know what to do.'

He started to ask her how, what were their numbers, but she opened the door again and squeezed through as though afraid to let something shut within escape. He looked at the phone and saw the little alphabetical plastic directory beside it. He went to it, moved the little lever to 'B' and pressed. The lid popped up, open and he saw the name 'Brownlow' neatly inscribed at the top of the list. He dialled.

*   *   *

162

'Robert? Don't be frightened. It's me, Karen. I've come to see you.'

His eyes were eerily open, fixed on the ceiling as though some fascination danced there. In spite of herself, Karen looked up, saw nothing but the pale, white flatness of it, not even the play of a shadow, a ripple of light. She leaned over him, forcing herself to smile and uselessly smoothed the bedclothes. She knew he had such 'quiet' periods. Mrs Luman had explained them to her when she was a girl and had come calling to ask if he would like to go for a walk.

'Not today, dear. He's having one of his quiet spells.'

It was partly the drugs, she knew, and partly because his damaged brain withdrew sometimes, when he could not cope. His head, she thought, was like a snail's shell. Coiled, safe and private within it, was the soft, grey malfunctioning brain. Moved, she put out her hand and touched his cheek, stroking it with one finger.

Tom knocked softly at the door, startling her. She snatched her hand away, embarrassed, hurried to prevent Tom coming in for a stranger might rouse Robert, upset him . . . Tom stepped back when she opened the door.

'What is it?'

'I've spoken to the Brownlow woman. She's on her way. She said she'd bring the other one . . . '

'Meg.'

'Yes.'

'I'd better stay with him. He's . . . sleeping,' she said, knowing no other word to explain his state, 'but if he wakes up . . . '

Tom nodded.

'OK. I'll wait here, keep an eye on her.' His words made Karen look down at Phyllis, who lay as they had found her. 'I wish that ambulance'd get a move on . . . ' He moved towards the door and Karen saw, beside the woman, the plastic bag.

'Give me the bag, will you? His costume.'

Tom looked around, saw it and handed it to her.

'I'd better get back to him,' she said. 'Thank you . . . '

Robert's eyes were closed now and he snuffled as though about to snore. Carefully, Karen drew a chair closer to the bed and sat down, placed the plastic bag on the ridge made by his legs. In the distance, she heard the wail of a siren. Its sound was drowned by that of a car drawing up, voices raised. Robert stirred, rolled his head. Karen began to talk, rapidly, to distract him, cover up the alarming noises of help arriving. She told him about the costume, her hand resting lightly on his chest, ready to restrain him.

They carried her out, covered with a red blanket. Paula Brownlow went with her, shouting instructions. For want of anything better to do, Tom picked up the pink quilt and replaced it on her bed, shaking and smoothing it into place. His eyes fell on the photograph in its polished silver frame. Phyllis was easily recognisable, even though he had only seen part of her face as she lay on the floor. The boy looked absolutely normal . . .

'Hello. Well, this is a bad business. Oh, sorry, let me introduce myself. Paul June.'

Tom shook his hand, explained again what had happened. Paul June thanked him, told him that they had been afraid of something like this.

'She's been under a terrible strain. She's such a devoted woman. She wouldn't hear of leaving poor Robert . . . '

With relief, Tom saw Karen over the rector's shoulder. She looked drained, shattered.

'Ah, Karen . . . My dear, what a terrible shock for you. But thank God you happened by. You and your friend here.'

Tom stood around, embarrassed as they talked. He was good in a crisis but impatient with the aftermath. He kept trying to catch Karen's eye, wondered if he could just walk out, sit in the car, but the hall was so small he would have to barge past them, excuse himself.

'Well, if there's nothing else I can do . . . '

'No, no. You've been marvellous. We're all so grateful to you both. Meg and I can cope now and Pansy's on her way . . . '

164

'I'll come by tomorrow and see how Robert is.'

'That's very kind, Karen. I'll be sure to tell Meg.' He turned to Tom and offered his hand again. 'Thank you so much.'

Tom put his arm around Karen's shoulder, felt her body trembling.

Paul June stood in the doorway, one hand raised, smiling at their backs as they went slowly down the path, between the rose-bushes.

Tom opened the door for Karen and helped her into the car. She sat with her hands upturned in her lap, staring straight ahead.

'Shall I take you somewhere for a cup of tea? Would you like to go to your parents . . . ?'

'No. Do you mind very much if we just go home?'

'No, of course not.' He leaned across her to fasten her seatbelt.

'I'm sorry. I've completely ruined your day.'

'Don't be daft. Thank God we came.'

'Yes. I don't know what would have happened if Robert had found her.' She shuddered and buried her face in his shoulder.

'It's all right, love. Everything's all right now. Come on. Let's go home.' He raised her face and kissed her cheek, whispering in her ear, 'And make love.'

At six that evening, Mrs Mitchell identified the sheeted body retrieved that morning from Brindsleigh Dam as that of her daughter, Lenora Gail Mitchell. She left the cold, disinfectant-smelling room sobbing, WPC Hignett supporting her. The autopsy could not begin but it was only a matter of routine. The pathologist had already told Riley that death was almost certainly due to strangulation – he had pointed to the marks on her neck – and it had not happened recently. He would fill in the details, Riley knew, though the precise time and place of death would be difficult, perhaps impossible, to determine. The twenty-fifth, Riley was prepared to bet, and somewhere between Passington riverside and Brindsleigh Dam where she had been dumped only when Luman had finished with her.

Then, at six fifteen, Superintendent Tait played his last card.

'No, Riley, I'm afraid not. I've given the matter very careful thought . . . '

'You can't do this,' Riley protested. 'We've got a body and enough circumstantial to bring Luman in. It's what we're bloody paid for. Our duty, if you like. Sir.'

'And bring him in we shall. Tomorrow morning . . . '

'Why wait for God's sake?'

'If you would sit down, Riley, and be calm, permit me to speak . . . '

'I'll stand,' Riley said. 'OK. Go on.'

'Thank you,' Tait said with heavy irony. 'I have not been idle this afternoon. I have been taking advice, legal advice, and I think you'll agree with me when you hear all the reasons, that we have opted for the wisest course. You see . . . ' Here he paused, summoning his old command, getting back, Riley thought, into his stride. But it won't wash this time, he promised himself. 'You see our difficulty is the publication of Miss Ashburton's drawing. That really was most unfortunate. I really do think we had better have an independent investigation into how that could have happened. But that's another matter. I mustn't keep you on tenterhooks any longer than is necessary. The point is, the public know that we have questioned Mr Luman already and they have seen a remarkably good likeness of him in their newspapers and on their television screens. They also know that he is – shall we say, mentally sub-normal? Now, the powers that be are most anxious, as I am, that there should be no suspicion, no hint of a possibility of our being accused of harassing a man who will almost certainly be judged incompetent to plead.' He paused, watching Riley through slitted eyes. Then he leaned forward, his tone and manner changing entirely. 'You know as well as I, Riley, that we are going to have the devil's own job bringing Luman to trial. All the cards are stacked against us. I am advised that the Chief Constable would be very . . . cross should we, even in-advertently, give the defence any more aces. I am led to believe that he will be positively furious should the Force be criticised in any way. These are delicate times, Riley. Very delicate times.'

'I don't understand, sir.'

'Yes you do, Riley. We do not want controversy and if Luman is our man, we want to nail him completely. Therefore, he must be seen by a competent, independent psychiatrist before we do anything. He must be assessed. We must be seen to do the right thing and, judging from the . . . er . . . débâcle last time you interviewed him, I think even you would welcome a few pointers as to how to get the best out of Mr Luman.'

'All right,' Riley said, 'where's the hitch?'

'There isn't one. Oh, of course, you will consider it inconvenient that no suitable psychiatrist is available until tomorrow morning, but that's a mere detail. It's all set up, I do assure you.'

'That's all right, sir. I can wait. On your orders.'

'How very co-operative of you, Riley. Those are, indeed, my orders.'

'So, what's the form?'

'Constable Smith will . . . collect, shall we say? . . . Mr Luman early tomorrow morning and take him to Oversleigh where Mr Jolley will observe his interview with the psychiatrist. Mr Jolley will then bring them both here and, to cut a long story short, you will have a free hand, Riley, a free hand. You will be the arresting officer, as you fully deserve to be.'

'I see.'

'You should be pleased. I think we can tie this one up very nicely, and all the credit will rebound on you. I think I can almost say, well done, Riley.'

'Thank you, sir. Thank you very much indeed.'

'Not at all, Riley. Not at all.'

Robert had not noticed the plastic bag when Karen placed it on the bed but waking to the full dark, shifting his legs, he felt and heard it slide to the floor. Robert held his breath and listened. There were no sounds, no wind in the trees or rain to patter against the windows. Robert stretched out his right arm, tapping the air with his flat palm until he felt the table, the bedside lamp. He made a throaty noise of protest as the light shocked his eyes. He waited, eyes shut, until his lids glowed yellow and it was safe to open them, safe to look. By then he had forgotten why he had put on the light. He frowned, puzzled, slowly eased himself up in the bed. His body felt old, his head heavy and not up to much. He began to get out of bed for that seemed to be the next step, the thing to do. His foot touched the plastic bag, retreated from its cold slipperiness. Curiosity made him bend over and peer, draw the bag towards him, pick it up. He opened it, stuck his nose and eyes into the aperture and saw only blue. A blue bright like the sky, like the hats Mam made him.

The costume, which seemed to unfurl itself from his clumsy hands like a silken banner was a wonder, a source of joy and beauty. He held the top in both hands, saw a great, cursive, scarlet R appliquéd to the chest. His chest.

'R-r-r-robert,' he said, his throat dry from sleep and long silence.

The R was red and made of some shiny material that caught the light and dazzled it back into his eyes. Robert crushed the top to his chest, snatched the trousers from the floor where they had fallen, hugged both pieces, rocking back and forth, crooning to himself with happiness. He sat so for a long time, his pleasure pure and uninterrupted, until the slow realisation that he could wear the suit bred an urgent, impatient desire to do so.

Robert transformed himself. The shirt gave him muscles and magic powers. The trousers bulged over his forgotten pyjama bottoms. He adjusted the mirror, turned this way and that. He could fly up to the ceiling, elongate his body to snatch a child from the path of a motor car half a mile away, further. He could be small and brave enough to enter a mouse's lair.

Well done, Robert!

His face fell. Reflected in the mirror, he saw himself wrong. He fought against the tears of disappointment, his face dissolving, re-forming. His face was not that of a superhero. His hat made him ordinary, worse. He turned away, ready to crawl

168

back into bed when he saw the plastic bag and pounced upon it, shaking it upside down with a kind of fury. A third piece of blue material fell onto the bed, was snatched up and eagerly examined. In winter, sometimes, Robert wore a Balaclava helmet. In his hands he recognised a similar garment, ending in a deep, shaped collar that should lie flat and smooth across his shoulders, dip to touch the uppermost curlicue of the emblazoned R. Teeth clenched to prevent them chattering with excitement, unable to stand still, Robert removed his woolly hat and pulled the hood over his head. At first he could not see at all, grunted with frustration, pulled and almost tore the material until, suddenly, the room appeared again before him. He tugged at the collar and his chin came free. He went to the mirror, his hands pressed to his face, opened his fingers little by little and peeped.

The blue hood, with a slight adjustment, framed the oval of his face from hairline to chin. It made his features chiselled, noble, his eyes a periwinkle blue. With gestures of love and care, Robert tweaked and smoothed the collar until it seemed to melt into the shirt and he stood tall, magnificent, other.

'Mam. Mam. Mam.' Robert blundered across the room, rattled the door open. 'Mam.' His shadow fell across the darkened hall, impaled on the oblong of light that fell from his open doorway. Robert felt for and found the light-switch. Mam's door was closed. Faintly, Robert realised that it was night, that he should not make a noise. He advanced on tiptoe, bent over, adapting his incredible body to smallness and silence. He opened Mam's door and pushed it slowly wide. He must not make a noise. He must show Mam the costume. The two ideas did not conflict in his head but made a simple harmony. He entered, stealthily. The light from the hall showed him the nightstand beside the bed, gleamed on the silver photo frame. Everything else lay in dark shadow. Robert remembered the reports then, forgot any other reason for being in the room. Carefully, he lowered his body to the carpet, on hands and knees crawled towards the cupboard. Reaching up, he traced the outline of the picture with his fingers and gently, gently, lifted it, shuffled on his knees to the corner of the room and placed it, safe, against the skirting board. Now! Robert turned too quickly, clumsy in his excited anticipation. His head cracked against the side of the nightstand and exploded with light. Robert fell back in terror, his mouth open in a silent scream.

Meg Sowers, waking, heart thumping, snatched at the dangling light-cord and sat up. What she saw, huddled against the wall, only a foot or so from her borrowed bed, was indescribable. She screamed.

What Robert saw, through the dazzle of light, the sharp, spreading pain in his head, looming up out of the bed above him was a monster. Fat pink plastic sausages coiled in her hair. Her cheeks were unnaturally sunken, her neck scrawny with wrinkles and slack skin.

'Robert? Is that you?'

Robert shrank from the strange voice, levered himself into a crouching position, ready to spring, run, hurl himself at her if necessary.

'Mam,' he said. 'Not Mam.'

'How dare you come barging in here? What time is it?' Meg fumbled for her watch, squinted at it. Robert began to inch towards the door. 'Whatever are you wearing?' For once, Meg Sowers's patience deserted her. This was too much. Perhaps Paula was right. Things were really getting out of hand. She swept back the bedclothes, fumbled for her slippers. Robert stood up then, a comic, pathetic apparition. Looking at him, his mouth hanging open, oozing saliva, in some silly blue hood, dressed like something out of a television commercial, she could not help laughing. It was in part reaction to her shock as well, she knew that. And then the laughter stopped. The ridiculous clothes also made him look sinister. A précis of recent events, suspicions and rumours flashed into her mind, making her heart trip and then beat too fast. 'I've had enough of this,' she said, standing. 'You get back to bed at once, young man, and take off that—'

Robert crashed into the door, hurled it against the wall from

170

which it rebounded and slammed. He had never been so afraid in his life. Mam was gone. Some monster occupied her place. He stood in the hall, not knowing what to do. The door opened behind him. He heard her voice, remembered her terrible, mocking laughter and the way it had died, like a light going out. He saw a door before him, the means of escape. He rattled the handle, his frightened hand slipping and the door opened the wrong way, outward.

'Robert, whatever are you doing . . . ?'

He stared, uncomprehending, into the cluttered cupboard. Wellington boots and the old, earth-stained smock Mam wore gardening. The mysteriously whirring electricity meter seemed to mock and chatter at him. Mam gone, no Mam. The monster's claw-like hand touched his shoulder as his eyes and then his hands found the axe.

In that split second, as his hands felt the smooth grain of the wood and his shoulders took the weight of its heavy, metal head, Robert became quite calm. He remembered he was a super-hero. The scarlet R glowed with a radiant power on his chest. He was capable of anything. He turned to face the monster, who held no terror for him now. He felt only hatred for her since she had witched Mam away and laughed at him. As she turned, he swung the axe high, its weight magnificent in his hands, its arcing movement a simple but beautiful extension of his body. The force of incredible powers flowed from him into the axe, which hung for a moment in the air, then descended, gathering speed.

Blood exploded from the staggering monster, a crimson splurge against the wall. As he swung the axe up again, Robert seemed to hear the world sigh:

Well done, Robert!

EPILOGUE

A small crowd had gathered, silent and orderly, outside the bungalow. More officers had arrived from Oversleigh, but one was sufficient to man the gate. Jolley approached on foot, from the police house, his smile still dimmed. He had telephoned Teddy Tait and his own station to cancel the scheduled interview with the psychiatrist, though it was thought that he would already have started out. Jolley had left his apologies. They would wheel on bigger fish now, he supposed, when they found Robert Luman. This was a detail, not his concern. Tait was sending a forensic team from Passington, and Riley. Jolley's work was finished here. He paused on the opposite side of the road. An elderly Mini cruised past, slowing out of curiosity, he guessed. He saw Hughes come out of the front door, followed by the still ashen-faced Smith. A competent man, Hughes. No need for Jolley to interfere. He put another man on the door. Quite right, Jolley approved. It was not necessary to make a man stand inside, amid the carnage. He saw Smith slope off towards the back garden, lighting a cigarette. He would be sure to put in a good word for young Smith. Nice wife. Lovely kiddy.

There was a ripple in the crowd. A tall blonde woman raised her voice. A girl with a jaunty bow in her hair approached the officer on the gate who bent a little stiffly to hear her. Jolley watched, distracted, outside it all. Nothing at all, really, to stop him sloping off back to Oversleigh. Hughes would hold the fort, hand over to Riley. Slowly, through the shock wave of what he had seen in that house and the pressing instinct to get away from it, to leave it all to others, Jolley recognised Karen Ashburton. He remembered her as a young tearaway of fifteen or so, a kid stretching her wings a little too enthusiastically for adult comfort. He began to cross the road just before the officer at the gate signalled to him. She used to be good with Robert Luman, he remembered, the nearest thing he had to a friend of his own, he supposed. Karen turned at his approach, her face anxious. Jolley nodded to her.

'This young lady says she's expected, sir.'

'Hello, Karen.' His natural smile hurt him a little as though, without it, his muscles had atrophied.

'Mr Jolley. What's going on?' He took her arm. Instinctively, she pulled against it, then relaxed, let him lead her a little way up the road, away from the craning crowd.

'What are you doing here?' he asked, sounding more officious than he liked or intended.

'I came to see how Robert is. I found Mrs Luman yesterday. They took her to hospital . . . '

'Yes,' he said, wondering who would break the news to Phyllis Luman, how.

'What's happened? Where's Robert? You lot aren't harassing him again, are you?' She looked very fierce and Jolley felt his smile return, sit on his face comfortably. For all it was inopportune, he could have hugged her.

'Let's get in,' he said, on impulse. They were standing beside his car.

'What for?'

'Let's talk. Please?'

She hesitated, biting her lower lip, then went around the car and got in. More slowly, having a care for his bulk, Jolley eased himself into the driving seat.

'Robert's gone,' he said, not knowing where else to start.

'Gone? Where? Robert wouldn't—'

'Karen, Karen, slow down. Don't go jumping to too many conclusions. You know me. You can trust me.'

'You're a policeman,' she said, sullen.

'And we're all tarred with the same brush,' he sighed. 'You used to know Robert Luman pretty well, get on with him.'

'Yes.'

'So maybe you can help us . . . me, now.'

'What do you mean, he's gone?'

173

'He's not in the bungalow. No sign of him.'

'Where's Meg Sowers? She was stopping with him. She must know . . .'

'Oh she's there all right. You won't like this, Karen. Mrs Sowers is dead.'

Karen turned to look at him. He knew what she was thinking, saw her slowly piece it together. She had seen the garden from the gate. He nodded once.

'Killed?'

'Yes. I'm afraid so.'

'But who would . . . You think Robert. Oh you lot are all the same.' She made to open the door, get out. Jolley caught her wrist, held it lightly but firmly.

'There is nothing to suggest anyone else. No forced entry, nothing. Now we have to find Robert quickly. If he didn't do it, he must be scared half to death. If he did do it, he's probably even more scared. Now, I happen to think it would be better for me to find him than have him hunted down by half the county force. You may not agree—'

'How do you know he isn't dead, too?'

'I don't. But you can understand that we have to make certain assumptions on the evidence to hand. Whatever happened, we have no reason to think Robert's dead. We have to find him, if only to rule him out.'

'Like you did last time, over Leni Mitchell.' Jolley decided to be prudent, to say nothing to this. He felt too tired and anxious and disgusted to get into a needless argument with her. 'I suppose you think this makes it a foregone conclusion that he killed Leni Mitchell. I saw on the news you'd found her.'

'The man's been close to two violent deaths. Coincidences do happen, but . . .' Jolley shrugged.

'He can't defend himself. He can't tell you—'

'Karen, the only person who can help Robert right now is his mother. She's not here. When she gets out of hospital she'll probably be in no fit state to help anyone, poor soul. Robert might have run off somewhere out of fear. Robert might have killed that poor woman. If you have any idea where he might be, you could save both of them a lot of pain.'

174

'I helped the police once,' Karen said bitterly, 'and all I did was to put them on to Robert, by accident. I don't want to do that again. I won't.'

'Robert's implicated by factual circumstances, girl. You wouldn't be doing anything except perhaps helping us to avoid a major police hunt—'

'That's what you're paid for, isn't it?' she flashed back at him.

'Very well.' Jolley deliberately leaned across her and opened the door. 'Thanks for your time.'

She caught her breath noisily. Her body tensed, seemed to flinch from contact with his arm. Jolley left the door open, straightened up.

'I don't know, not for sure. I won't tell you what I think.' She elbowed the door wide and scrambled out. 'If you – just you, mind – want to follow me, I think I know where he might be.'

Jolley nodded once and she slammed the door. He watched her hurry back down the road, waited. He ought to tell someone but if he did she'd back out. It seemed to him important, the very least he could do, to find Robert if he could. For decency's sake and Phyllis Luman's.

The old Mini came slowly past. She glanced at him. He let her get to the corner, her indicator flashing, before he started his own car and carefully drew out, following her, but not obviously.

Jolley knew Lulford, of course, had brought the kids there once on a picnic when it first opened. They'd been bored, he remembered, ready to fly the coop, had come, probably, out of a sense of duty to the family, knowing that soon such impositions could not be placed upon them. At that time he had been more worried about Eileen, how she would cope with the kids off to college and training courses. They had walked together by the lake and she had reassured him, as she always did. He was, amazingly, enough for her. Her devotion to the kids, though total and deeper than expression could fully admit, had been a kind of detour. They had, without them, picked up their life together at the point where James's birth had

175

interrupted it. With changes, of course . . . Only last summer he had escorted Eileen, a little reluctantly, he admitted, to a craft fair here and had found it a tacky, gimcrack affair, but she, with her infallible nose, had rootled out a few pretty bargains, had enjoyed herself.

When he was a lad, Lulford Towers had been a decaying mansion, glimpsed only from the road. Jolley was hazy about its transformation into a country park, the whole estate being managed now by some faceless board or conglomerate. It was part of the new leisure industry, whatever that was. But the grounds were now kempt and tidy. There were a restaurant and public conveniences, a children's farm and a gift shop in the stable block. He remembered a flurry of excitement a couple of years back when the BBC had used the exterior of the house as a background to some historical drama series he had subsequently dozed through. The house, for reasons he did not know, was still shuttered and closed, though no longer obviously decaying.

He followed Karen Ashburton's slow Mini past the signs to a designated car park, up to the stable block where she parked on the grass verge. He stopped behind her. Mid-week, mid-morning, an overcast morning at that, the place had a deserted, withdrawn air about it. Beside the ornate, hand-painted sign to the gift shop, was a rotund, mechanical metal pony, perched on a flexible pediment. *Broncobuster* was stencilled across its flaking scarlet base. *10p a ride.*

He saw Karen get out of the Mini, pause, go back to the car and lock her shoulder bag inside. He removed his keys and climbed out. She stood, hands in her jacket pockets, waiting for him. The mountain must go to Mahomet, he thought.

'I don't *know*,' she stressed. 'It's only a hunch. I used to bring him here sometimes when I was a kid. He always liked it here. A couple of times lately I've said to Mrs Luman, maybe he'd like to come here with me again. He may have heard or she may have mentioned it to him. When a thing's in Robert's head . . . ' Her voice faded on a suspicion of tears.

'You haven't seen him lately, then?'

'No. He wasn't very well when I called . . . Your lot,' she said, bitter again.

Jolley drew himself up, looked around. The ground sloped gently to the river, stretched in flat, open parkland to the left. On the right, in the distance, the enclosures, sheds and paddocks of the farm.

'It's a big place,' he said, thinking it would take a lot of men to really scour the park. Off in the distance were woods . . .

'He had his favourite spots,' Karen said. 'I suggest we split up . . . ' He looked at her, alert and guarded at once. 'Oh, don't worry. I won't do anything heroic. I'll bring him to you if I find him.' Jolley considered, nodded.

'Whatever happened to that lad?' he asked suddenly, for no other reason than to establish some real contact with her. 'The one you were going with when we first met? The one your parents didn't approve of.'

'He's dead,' she said bluntly, even, he thought, cruelly. 'Came off his motorbike on the A604. Why?'

'I'm sorry. Just trying to—'

'Don't,' Karen said. It was a warning. 'Robert used to like the old boathouse. Do you know it?' Jolley nodded. 'And the woods beside it. There's a picnic area. He used to like that. We used to eat our sandwiches there, always. I'll go this way.' She struck off immediately, towards the farm.

It was crazy, Jolley knew. He would be a laughing stock when this came out. Well, it wouldn't be the first time and his skin was thick. The thing was, he trusted Karen Ashburton. His police work had always been based on a degree of trust and he was too old now to change. 'You couldn't change if you tried,' Eileen always said and he smiled at the thought of her, trudging down towards the river, veering left. He had already lost sight of Karen.

The old boathouse no longer existed in any viable sense. The offshore wall stood, its arched doorway open to the river. Three steps led down to the sloping earth. A little of the slipway remained, green and treacherous with weed. It was empty except for a discarded can of Lilt. He turned left again,

177

following the path along the bank. Trees soon forced him inland. The undergrowth was thick beneath them. It would take a lot of men with sticks and billhooks, probably, to search this lot thoroughly. But then they weren't looking for anything concealed, he reminded himself. Yesterday they had found their body in the dam, this morning an extra, unexpected one, or the constituent, hacked parts of one. The trees opened in that natural-accidental way trees have, to form a clearing. Rustic tables with benches attached were set about, inviting people to rest, picnic. It was deserted, forlorn, somehow. Jolley resisted the impulse to rest himself, trudged on. The whole thing was hopeless, he felt, his spirits sagging.

Karen thought she had started a wild-goose chase and was partly glad, partly embarrassed. She had visited every nook and cranny of the children's farm, walked up among the pens of Highland cattle and goats, had stood and watched the sad-looking donkeys. She had gone on to the high point, overlooking the whole park, where Robert had liked to sit and gaze, pointing at people, cars. She hesitated at the gate to the pinetum. Her explorations had brought her back in sight of the parked cars and had Jolley been visible she would have called off the search there and then. The only thing Robert had ever liked about the pinetum was its name. She had not understood why this sent him into peals of giggles until Mrs Luman had explained that he saw it as two words: 'pine' and 'tum'. As she slid back the metal bolt, the 'joke' seemed weaker than ever, almost sour. No, the pinetum with its razored lawns and carefully labelled trees held no charms for Robert. It was a quiet, special place. Ball games and dogs were forbidden. Even on busy bank holidays it seemed to attract the serious visitor or to enjoin upon the frivolous an air of hushed contemplation. Karen liked it, had often sketched there alone. Now she walked it with her own heavy thoughts, sparing only sideways glances at the carefully nurtured trees.

This protected enclosure was shaped like half a bowl, its furthermost and lowest boundary being formed by the lake.

The handsome stretch of black water was now used as a breeding ground for waterfowl and a sagging, not very daunting wire fence, marked at intervals with red warning signs, ran along the edge of the pinetum's green smooth lawn. For lack of anything better to do, postponing the moment of return, Karen paced the fence, looking out at the water. This route would bring her, eventually, back to the gate, the cars, Jolley. She did not, for a moment, consider that Jolley might have found Robert. If he was here, she would find him.

Just before the fence ended and the ground began to slope upward, through trees, to the gate, a broken rustic bridge stood at the water's edge, connecting the bank to an islet a few yards square. Robert sat, child-like, in the middle, his legs stuck out in front of him, a brightly coloured comic spread across his knees. More comics were beside him and on the bridge, their pages tattered and the worse for wear. Also near him was a manila folder blown open by the breeze. Sheets of yellowing paper, marked by black printing, a variety of handwritings shifted and rustled.

Karen stopped short of him, a little behind him. Her surprise was quick and passing. She had, after all, known that he would be here. She felt no triumph or pleasure, either. It occurred to her at once that she could creep away, tell Jolley she had drawn a blank. That way she could give Robert a little time, a chance to get away. Had she been thinking of anyone but Robert, there might have been some hope in this, but her next immediate thought was that Robert could not fend for himself. He would wait here, probably until he grew bored or cold or hungry and then wander out, vulnerable, confused . . . Besides, he was wearing the ridiculous suit she had made for him which, of itself, cancelled any chance of his passing unnoticed. There was nothing for it but to do as she had promised to do. She walked forward.

'Robert?' He looked up from his comic but straight ahead, did not turn his head towards her. She took a few more steps along the fence. 'Robert? It's me, Karen. Hello, Robert.' He looked up at her then, his jaw slack and moist in the framing blue hood. The effect of the hood, she saw, was to make him ageless, an old baby.

'Ka-ren,' he said and gurgled.

'Yes. It's me. Hello.'

'Ka-ren.' His voice was warm with recognition and pleasure. With one of those sudden bursts of energy she remembered, he scrambled up, scattering comics heedlessly, and jogged across the bridge. She saw some of the sheets of paper flip from the folder and float, swaying on the water. 'Ka-ren.'

'Careful,' she said. 'Let me help you.' He had got one leg over the sagging fence, seemed unable to lift the other. She went closer to him, seeing for the first time the dark brown, ugly stains on his costume. The largest absorbed the R, dulled it almost to black. 'Here, let me help.' He put one arm over her left shoulder, leaning on her and she bent, tugging at his trousers, trying to lift the leg over the fence. She remembered his limp, thought that it must have grown worse again. Or perhaps he had injured himself in his flight. His pyjamas showed, muddied, below the blue trousers. His knee bent and she lifted his leg over the fence. He made a sound like laughter and he staggered against her, throwing his other arm around her in a fierce hug.

'Ka-ren.'

She braced herself against his weight, swayed. She closed her eyes, held on to him, feeling sick. She knew without being told or examining too closely that the smell that came from him was that of blood. She hugged him hard as best she could, slowly drew away from him, breathing through her mouth.

'Are you all right?' she said. He nodded happily, his grin slipping, returning. 'What a good job I found you, eh? Come on, now. You must be cold.' She reached for his hand, for so they had always walked together, linked, but he held back.

'Where?'

'I'm going to take you . . . ' She stopped, looking into his eager eyes. She could not lie to him, especially not now. 'I'm going to take you back,' she said carefully. 'My car's just up there . . . ' She pointed towards the gate and beyond. Robert slipped his hand into hers.

'Ride,' he said happily.

'That's right,' she agreed, setting off up the slope, the backs of her knees aching. 'I'll take you for a ride.'

He came with her, docile, his comics and papers forgotten. At the gate Karen let go of his hand and manipulated the bolt. It slid back with a dull crash of metal and the hinges squeaked as she pushed the gate open. She led him through, turned to fasten the gate as the notice requested.

'All right, now, Robert? Come on.'

She could see Jolley but he had not noticed them. He was resting his backside against the bonnet of his car, munching a bar of chocolate from which, with each bite, he tore a little of the red and silver wrapping. He reminded her of a voracious squirrel.

'Ride,' Robert said loudly and pointed.

'Yes. In a minute. I promise.'

'Ka-ren.'

Jolley heard their voices, stopped eating, pushed his heavy body away from the car. He stood, silhouetted against the light, watching their slow, incongruous approach. The light behind him made it impossible for Karen to read his expression. She led Robert from the grass onto the metalled road. He was limping quite badly, dragging one leg. They came up to Jolley who, almost guiltily, Karen thought, stuffed the remains of the chocolate bar into his pocket.

'Ride,' Robert shouted and broke free of her hand.

She and Jolley were both startled, both took an instinctive step forward as though to restrain him. Both stopped, looking at each other, the trust between them stretched taut and fragile.

Robert ran awkwardly, dragging his leg, in a sort of swaying bounce toward the plump, stylised metal pony. He slapped its small saddle with both hands, making it rock.

'Ride,' he demanded.

Slowly, the tension drained out of Karen. She began to walk towards Robert, pushing her hands into her pockets. Jolley followed her, caught her up.

181

'Good God,' he said softly. In the full light, Robert's costume looked ghoulish, the extent of the staining clearly visible.

'Ka-ren. Ride,' he repeated, his voice rising to a whine, shuffling his feet with excitement and frustration.

'Let him,' Karen said, not looking at Jolley.

Jolley hesitated a moment then walked forward, his hand fishing in his trouser pocket. Robert unsteadily, excitedly, climbed onto the undersized pony, grasping the stiff metal reins. Jolley bent and inserted ten pence into the arrowed metal slot. At once the machine began to thump and squeak. Robert was thrown backwards, forwards, lifted into the air. His excited, happy laughter rose above the clanking of the machine. Karen and Jolley watched in silence.

POSTSCRIPT

Kerry Mather stood at the edge of Lulford Lake, disappointed. Nowhere had it said that the lake was available for fishing, but looking at a map of the area he had assumed that such a stretch of water, in a designated country park, would be open to fishermen. Now he read again the sign proclaiming the lake *Private*, a breeding reserve for wildfowl and felt that he had had a wasted journey.

It had been the frequent mention of Brindsleigh in the newspapers of late that had prompted him to look at the map. He was hazy about the precise location of Brindsleigh Dam which, in truth, held no interest for him now. Indeed he would probably have forgotten all about it had it not been for the 'savage axe murder' in the village, following close on the finding of Leni Mitchell's body. The two events were naturally linked in everybody's mind and the village had become something of a tourist curiosity. Kerry Mather had no intention of visiting the village to join the vulgar, gawping throng, but looking at the map and noticing the country park so close by, he thought a day out there, some fishing, would make a change. By chance, Muriel, his mother and Donald, his father were entertaining some old friends, business colleagues of his father's that bank holiday and did not need the car. He knew that the offer of the car was made primarily because they did not want him around when their friends came. His unemployed state, what his father now referred to as his 'unemployability' or 'uselessness' embarrassed them. He did not mind. He was glad of a chance to get out, be by himself.

He almost completely believed now, as did everyone else, that the 'mad axeman of Brindsleigh', who had been taken into custody by the police, was also responsible for Leni Mitchell's death. He felt no qualm or tug of personal involvement when his mother tutted over the tragedy and prompted his father's fulminations against such 'animals'. He could join in quietly, with nods and grunts of assent, all that was required of him. A couple of times, out of some perverse instinct, he had tried to think about it, to explore for himself and in detail the connection between the motiveless slaughter of an old woman in a bungalow and the strangulation of a schoolgirl, but when he did so a terrible boredom descended on him, a feeling of restless impatience, a desire, he thought, to think of nicer, more constructive things. He sighed heavily.

The noise made a couple – middle-aged, properly dressed in tweeds and stout walking shoes, who were closely examining one of the showpieces of the pinetum – pause and turn to look at him. Kerry Mather, embarrassed, shrugged and began to move away, up the slope towards the gate. Being a bank holiday, the country park was crowded. He let himself out into a world of loud voices, scampering, squealing children, adults laughing and taking photographs. Beyond the children's farm which he had already explored, which was now thronged by people peering and poking and laughing witlessly at the penned and caged beasts, was a caravan park, filled with predominantly white wheeled homes. He had been there, too, and had stood watching a woman peg dripping, brightly coloured clothing on an improvised line while children ran around her, teasing a young dog. He set his back to the farm and the caravan site and struck off towards the car park, moving more quickly than anyone else around him, ignoring all but the strolling lovers, of whom there seemed to be a great many. He looked sadly into the back of the car when he reached it at his fishing tackle. There was time, of course, to drive on somewhere, find a place on the riverbank, but somehow the will to do so was dull in him. He took the plastic box of sandwiches, the Thermos flask, and carried them slowly down to the old boathouse. Beside it, a man sat on a canvas stool, his line dangling lifeless in the water.

'Any good?' Kerry Mather asked, thinking that he might, after all, and without further driving, try his luck.

'No,' the man said, scratching his hairline under his flat cap.

'Too many people about. Kids swimming up there.' He jerked his head to the left, indicating the general direction. Kerry nodded and moved away.

The path soon left the riverbank, forced away by trees. Kerry Mather entered a little wood, the sound of splashing, girlish squeals and boyish bravado reaching him muffled by the screening trees. Where they thinned, he saw the glitter of water in sunlight, the flash of bodies. He walked on until he came to a clearing, a natural one, very green in the sunshine. A rustic table, with attached benches, stood off to one side, inviting. He carried his food there, sat and began to eat. Sunday's cold chicken in a pap of white bread. He poured coffee into the plastic mug and watched the steam rise, let it stand to cool. He heard voices other than those of the invisible swimmers.

'Aw, come on, Deb.'

'No. I told you.'

'Please.' The tone was pleading, disappointed.

They came in sight, the girl still in the act of shrugging off the boy's arm. They did not notice Kerry Mather set off to one side of the clearing, quietly chewing. The boy's body was very white in bright blue swimming trunks. His short, dark hair was plastered in a fringe to his forehead. He stopped suddenly.

'I'm going to get changed then. It's cold.'

'Suit yourself,' the girl said with a slight and certainly unconscious toss of the head. She wore a white sleeveless blouse and pink shorts which stretched taut over her rump.

'I'll see you back at the caravan site, then,' the boy called. 'OK?'

'Yes. I'm going there now.'

The boy saw Kerry Mather then and stared at him, frowning, flushing slightly. He turned and scampered back the way he had come, looking cold and frustrated. The girl passed through the clearing. Kerry Mather watched her. At its edge, she left the path, stepped, at first gingerly, then with growing confidence among the undergrowth. He saw her duck her head, her thick, loose hair swinging out from her head, as she passed into shadow, under a low branch.

Kerry Mather chewed and swallowed. He sipped the coffee and finding it cool enough, swallowed half of it, washing down the sticky bread. He thought about the conversation he had overheard. The girl was walking away from the caravan site. He became anxious suddenly. His hand trembled as he set the mug down. Furthermore, she had left the designated path. He stared at the point among the trees where he had last seen her. She would return, of course, realising her mistake. Or the boy would come back, looking for her. Without really meaning to, Kerry Mather found himself repacking the plastic box, snapping its lid in place. He was standing, his knees bent uncomfortably because of the bench attached to the legs of the table. He tossed the remains of the coffee into the undergrowth, shook the mug and screwed it back in place on top of the Thermos. He stepped over the bench, feeling very worried now, even alarmed, tucking the box and flask under his arm. The girl might be lost, he thought, evidently did not know her way around. He hurried across the clearing, stopped for a moment to look back across it, down the path he and they had entered by, along which the boy had gone when he left her. Then quickly but cautiously, Kerry Mather stepped into the wood, ignoring the path and went in search of the girl, to see if she was all right.